NIMBLEFOOT THE ANT
Her Adventures

VYTAS TAMULAITIS

NIMBLEFOOT
THE ANT

Her Adventures

Translated from the Lithuanian by
ALBINAS BARANAUSKAS
and CLARK MILLS

Illustrated by
PRANAS LAPÉ

MANYLAND BOOKS, INC. : NEW YORK

CONTENTS

1. THE TOWN OF THE BLACK ANTS

In the anthill, under the Big Fir, great things were astir. There the season of spring brought with it hard labor. From early dawn till late at night, thousands of black ants hurried through the streets of the town. Some rolled huge logs—pine-needles or stalks of dry grass—to build new dwell-ings; others, wiping sweat from their foreheads, dragged heavy boulders of gravel to repair the streets, or came back from the woods laden with food, which they handed out to other hungry laborers.

5

On the outskirts, under the grass and ferns, engineers were busy excavating for new highways, along which enough food had to be carried not only for the others, but for rainy days and to last through the whole winter.

As in every large city, the streets were full of busy people rushing on, each with his own purposes and cares. A curious man would look in vain for a loafer: not one stood idle at a streetcorner, although no one was there to remind such a creature of his duties. Not even a policeman watched over public order. There was no need for him.

"What a wonderful town! How the little ones always agree among themselves!" often exclaimed Mrs. Squirrel on a branch of the fir, shelling a nut. "And they don't even work for themselves— they drag loads, and hurry, and suffer for the sake of others—for the whole town! . . ."

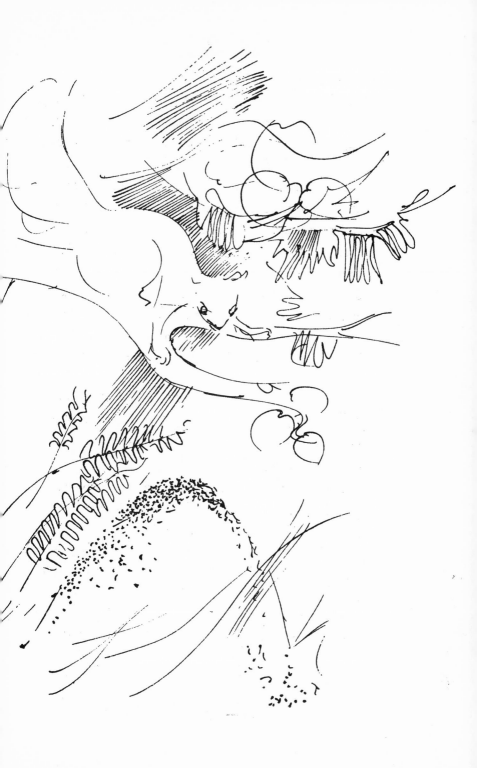

No matter how busy the laborers, the engineers, and the road teams, none bore such a heavy burden as the old nurse, Hustle-Bustle. At the end of the day her head ached and her ears buzzed with fatigue. She had to care for all the babies and children of the town. She fed them, trained them, and took them out every day, to walk in the fresh air and to sunbathe. She had to be everywhere, see everything, hear everybody. True, she had maids to help her, but the responsibility was all hers; she didn't expect anyone else to do her work. As soon as she'd bring a cup of milk to one of the tiny ones, another would clamor for a song, and a third, his mouth sad, would complain that no one ever told him a fairy tale.

All through the day the old nurse had to run from one to another. She even had to go into the pasture to milk the cows, so that the little ones could have fresh milk.

In summer, the town's herd grazed nearby on blades of grass, and spent the winter in stalls inside the anthill. The cows were little, greenish insects that we call "aphids." They supplied the ants with a sweet, nutritious beverage, and the ants, in return, cared for them as if they were domestic creatures.

Only late at night, when she had tucked the

mischief-makers away in their beds and lulled them to sleep, could the old nurse relax. Then she would climb out to the top of the hill. From there she could see the woods looming everywhere in the dark and listen to the song of the nightingale— loud, clear, and filled with the longings of a summer night. And she could see the dark blue sky overhead, filled with bright, twinkling stars, or watch the white moon pour its bluish light over all the world. Silence lay on all things—beautiful and so still that the joys and sorrows of her youth would come crowding back into her mind.

On the evening of the day that begins our tale of the strange adventures of a little ant, Hustle-Bustle again stood on her anthill, listening to the songs of the grasshoppers and thinking of a not-too-distant past, when the town had been attacked by plundering hordes of the red ants. Yet it seemed long ago. Since then, the town had grown and had trained more soldiers to defend it. And after the destruction, many new laborers had rebuilt it, larger and more beautiful than before. Of course, it had cost long days of toil, with heavy logs on their backs and food in their hands, but not a single ant had complained that he was tired or overworked.

As the old nurse thought of these things, suddenly she heard in the still night the hurried steps of a guard. A harsh military voice called out at the gate:

"Halt! Who goes there?"

Old Hustle-Bustle tuned her ears. Who could it be? Visitors rarely came, and strangers almost never. Yet if some orphaned insect or a lost traveller knocked on the gate at night, in the rain or during a storm, he would always find shelter and a friendly welcome. But the weather was clear and the sky bright with moonlight; one could spend the night anywhere. Was it a beggar? But then, why so late? The old nurse got up to have a look, herself, at the sudden guest. What was her amazement when she saw a red ant, armed with a pair of strong sharp claws, standing at the gate!

"What do you want?" asked the guard, his dagger at the ready.

"I've lost my way in the dark," stammered the red ant. "I did, really; please let me rest here a while. And if you will, a bite to eat. . . ."

Who could know if the red ant was telling the truth?

"Nurse," said one of the guards, "you've seen a lot in your long life. What should we do with this stranger?"

"Please, please, take pity on an unlucky creature! I fell into an ant lion pit and almost had my head taken off. I'm wounded. It's so hard to travel by night. . . . How can I find my way? You black ants are famous for your hospitality—don't turn me away . . ."

"And you red ants are well known—for your ingratitude," coldly replied Hustle-Bustle. "You rob and steal. You even attacked our town."

"But can I, alone as I am, hurt you? And besides," he wheedled, 'I belong to a most correct family of red ants. We aren't robbers at all. Please help me!"

It's true, said Hustle-Bustle to herself, what could one ant do to the town, even if he were a robber? He was limping, and he seemed to be wounded. Hustle-Bustle felt pity stir in her breast.

"I'll take care of him, myself," she said to the guards.

She took the stranger inside, gave him something to eat, and let him sleep in the guest room. But she didn't sleep that night at all. Tossing restlessly, she wondered why the red ant had looked so sharply and curiously about him, and why he'd kept asking questions about everything he saw. Then, too, it was plain he'd overdone his complaints about his bad luck, just as he'd been too honey-tongued when he praised the hospitality and

11

way of life of the black ants. Feeling strangely uneasy, Hustle-Bustle got up shortly before dawn and
quietly tiptoed into the room where her guest was
sleeping. The room was empty. The red ant was
gone.

Hustle-Bustle ran to the guards at the gate. They
told her they hadn't seen anyone leave the town.
At once a reinforced guard set roadblocks in every
street, and searched through every corner of the
anthill. The red ant, it seemed, had melted into
the air without a trace. No one had seen him go,
and nobody had an idea who he might have been.

2. THE SPY

In the center of the black, enormous woods lived
a tribe of red robber ants. At this time they were
ruled by a fearless, cruel chieftain named Iron Jaw
the Bad-Tempered.

Their stronghold was a cavern under the rotten
stump of an aspen-tree by a little clearing full of
blueberry bushes, overshadowed by branches of
tall pines. Here grew most of the poisonous, ugly
forest herbs, which made the approaches to the
robbers' lair seem even more sinister. No insect,
bug, or beetle came near the spot, since none
wanted to perish at the hands of the robbers. (The
red ants were pitiless, even beyond their dreadful
repute.)

The red robbers were members of the indus-
trious, respectable ant family, but they were the
greatest idlers and loafers in the world. The only
occupation they enjoyed was robbing and killing.
Nature had made them dangerous—and brave.
They had great military skill, and were well armed
with huge pairs of razor-sharp claws. Slaves, prisoners of war, or children of the black ants did all
their work. A gang of robbers would march out
into the woods, conquer the towns of black ants,
snatch their eggs, and bring them back to the
cavern. Here the red ants would hatch them and
raise slave-children to do the work, while they ate
their fill and lay about in the sun. The robbers
were even too lazy to eat; they had to be fed! The
slaves had to gather the food, chew it up, and place
it in their masters' mouths.

A road led from the robbers' underground fort,
under the thick grass, into the mysterious woods.
Along this way the robbers would march out to
the wars or return in victory, driving before them
hundreds of slaves laden down with rich booty.

The simple flowers that grew beside the clearing felt lonely and forgotten. Never did a visitor
come, never a beetle climb their stems to swing on
their leaves, never a bee pause for a chat: the robbers' lair was there. Week after week they stood,

alone and dejected. Only, without fail, the morning dew collected on them.

On this bright summer afternoon the clearing lay still, and dismal. A dandelion's fuzzy head turned to the ground, a wild poppy trembled and shook, as if expecting something terrible to happen at any moment. The robbers' cavern lay still, ominous. No red ant yawned in the sunshine or shouted at the slaves. Guards at the entrance spoke in whispers, or kept a sharp watch on the road that led into the woods.

And then, there in the shadows of the distant ferns, a red ant appeared. In his haste he stumbled often, tottering in his fatigue. He came closer, and one could see that he had made a dangerous, long journey.

The guards sighted him and a great tumult rose at the gate. Some rushed out into the road to meet him.

"Tell us the news, now!" they cried, even before they reached him.

The red ant wiped the sweat from his forehead and cast a shrewd, haughty glance at his curious fellows.

"Where's the Chief?" he asked, grimly.

"He's been waiting a long time for you."

"Go tell him I'm back."

Everyone hurried into the cavern.

"Leader, great Leader, the scout has returned!" shouted the robbers, pounding on the stone door of the chieftain's quarters.

"Bring him in," answered a deep voice from inside.

The red ant disappeared behind the massive door. This was the "wounded" visitor to the town of the black ants, who had so strangely disappeared on a moonlit night.

3. THE SECRET COUNCIL

The snare drums rattled such a wild tattoo on the ramparts of the robbers' castle that the leaves of shrubs trembled on every side, and a peapod burst open from the shock.

"What terrible noise is that?" wondered a butterfly, trembling on a spike of hair-grass. "They must have gone mad! Such an uproar even at midday, when everyone sweetly dozes in the warm sun!"

"No good will come of it," said a red-spotted fly from a fern-leaf. "When the robbers begin beating their drums, soon even the earth will tremble." And opening her wings, she vanished beyond a tree. The butterfly followed, her large wings fluttering and shimmering in the sun, till she disappeared in some juniper branches.

The drumming stopped, and after an uneasy silence the bugles sounded, summoning all the robbers into the hall of the Secret Council to hear of great, fateful decisions.

At one end of the hall, on an upturned acorn-cup, sat a giant red ant with an enormous pair of strong, evil-looking claws. It was Iron Jaw the Bad-Tempered himself. His red beard was longer than that of any robber, and his angry eyes flashed. From his throne, the acorn-cup, he proclaimed his decrees, which brought sorrow and disaster to many wood-dwellers. About the throne lay an ankle-deep carpet made of many silken insect-wings, costly and as soft as down.

Iron Jaw held in his right hand a scepter fashioned from a grasshopper's leg. From it hung the head of a spider—symbol of his power of life and death over all insects, bugs, and beetles. Behind him crowded his old warriors, now ennobled for their past courage and skill in battle. The red ant, still tired from his journey, stood before the throne.

"Speak!" said Iron Jaw. "And all of you, listen! We are ready to make a decision," he added, striking his chest.

"Great Leader!" began the red ant. "I found the town and asked for shelter. I pretended I was wounded and lost, but they didn't want to believe me. When all were asleep, I scouted the place thoroughly. It's a rich city, crammed with goods of all kinds. Great herds of cows are pastured nearby, and the warehouses are filled with curdled milk and dry cheeses. Under the weight of gnat hams and salted earthworms the shelves sag. The black ants have even hired trash removers—little ones who devour everything the ants discard. And that isn't all! They have professional winemakers, little yellowish bugs who produce such a sweet wine that the heart melts at the first sip. . ."

"I must taste that wine," thundered Iron Jaw, smacking his lips.

"And I! And we!" roared the robbers, making the whole cavern quake.

"The best time to attack is now," continued the red ant, "since the workers have breached the wall to drag in a large earthworm. If we go through that break, we'll be close to the nurseries. With their thousands of eggs and larvae, we can swell the ranks of our slaves. It shouldn't even be too hard to force our way through the gate—the winter's damage there hasn't yet been fully repaired. And at another spot in the wall some missing pine-needles leave a gap that they haven't finished closing with clay and resin. Two or three of us could jump through and easily widen it. The wall is high, but once we beat off the first counter-attack, we could break it on both sides of the main gate. Then we'd have the town surrounded by an iron ring of our troops, and no one could get away."

"Splendid!" roared Iron Jaw. "You've performed our mission well. In recognition, I confer on you the Order of the Red Fly of the Agaric Mushroom. You shall stand beside me when we storm the town. And you, my lads," he added to the crowd, "all of you know what's in store for us tomorrow: death, or hundreds of new slaves and great jars of sweet wine! Our slave-supply is low; soon it will be too small to allow us to enjoy our leisure in the sun. Forward, loyal subjects, to battle! I, Iron Jaw the Bad-Tempered, have spoken."

"Long live our great Leader!" shouted the robbers.

"The town of the black ants must be taken!"

"And its people, our prisoners and slaves!"

Iron Jaw rose to his feet. Guards pushed wide the door (a copper hornet's wing), and stood at attention as he left the hall. The robbers followed, scattering through all the castle.

Shadows soon glided into the clearing and surrounded the stump of the aspen-tree, which again stood silent. One would think nobody was there.

22

That night, if you had walked through the clearing, you would have seen only a small, insignificant
clump of ferns off to one side.

4. THE RED ANTS ON THE MARCH

Before sunrise, all the robbers stood in formation at the gate. Ready to march, they waited for the Leader to appear. Soon, haughty and grim, he came and lifted his right foreleg. The whole army was now in motion, strung out along the even road that led into the woods. In time with their heavy pace, the robbers began their song of war:

> *Onward, on, into the fray!*
> *What the danger we should fear?*
> *Who could dare to bar our way?*
> *Ranks, brave ranks of robbers here!*

They marched across the clearing, then, skirting the blueberry bushes, plunged into the dark
woods.

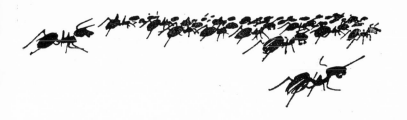

They moved in closed ranks, for they were real
soldiers. A tremendous force was on the march.
They looked brave and ferocious; each was armed
with a pair of strong, sharp claws. They inter-
rupted their singing with hoarse shouts and wild
threats. Their angry cries frightened all the small
creatures of the woods, who were afraid to look.

"Run, save yourselves, run for your lives,"
called a cockchafer, wakened by the song, as he
scrambled to the topmost branch of a juniper-bush.

Soon, hidden by hummocks of moss, the robbers
were out of sight. But for a long time their song
rang out, until it faded in the distance.

25

A little brook trickled from the bushes below a hillock, across the army's route. The first ranks came upon it, broke formation, and scattered along its bank, hoping to find a bridge. They found none, and had no time or wish to build one for themselves. Iron Jaw came up and gazed across the water. Many water-flies dashed over the surface on their long, spidery legs. They were known mostly as "the Ferrymen."

"You there, come, ferry us across," called out Iron Jaw."

"And what will you pay us?" laughed one Ferryman.

"We might eat you!" shot back Iron Jaw.

"That's little profit for us." said another Ferryman, yawning. And with one glide he darted to the opposite bank.

"With these jokes, you'll end up in a bad way," said Iron Jaw sharply. "Do you expect us to build a bridge? All right, but then, as soon as we get to the other side, not one of you will be alive. You'll all end up here," he added, patting his round belly.

"But there are so many of you!" said the first Ferryman respectfully. It was clear that Iron Jaw's threat had completely cowed him and his comrades.

The Ferrymen, too, had heard much about this robber tribe. They knew, for instance, that the

red ants never left undone what they had set out
to do.

"Make up your minds, you fools!" roared Iron
Jaw, in a passion. "Will you ferry us across? I give
you as long to think it over as it takes to com-
mand my soldiers!"

"We will, sir, we will. But on condition that
you not eat us," answered an elderly water flea as
he sailed toward the robber army, followed by his
friends.

"All right, agreed. Robber's word of honor.
That is, if you obey orders, of course. Now, let's
go!"

All the water fleas thereabout steered to the
bank. The robbers climbed on their backs or clung
to their legs, almost a platoon on each one. The

Ferrymen put their hearts in it, and were across in a flash. In another moment the second party was over. All went smoothly till the end, when Iron Jaw suffered a painful experience.

The chieftain and his nobles were the last to cross. Their Ferryman, young and without experience, was quite exhausted. As he reached the middle of the brook, where the water was deepest, he paused to catch his breath.

"Come on! What d'you think you're doing?" hissed Iron Jaw, lifting his claw to strike.

In his panic, the young fellow dived straight for the bottom. Iron Jaw and his cronies were left thrashing in the water.

"Get him! Get him!" gasped Iron Jaw, his head half under water. One of his aides and two nobles had already sunk from sight. But the robbers didn't let their chieftain perish so easily. A whole swarm leaped into the brook to save him and his suite. Joined one to another in a living chain, they paddled into the brook, fished out Iron Jaw and his generals, and carried them to land. The first words of the Leader were shrill:

"Catch that water dog!"

But this wasn't so easy. All the Ferrymen, who had seen the ducking of the robber leaders, were gone in a flash. They crouched in safe places that only they knew, and it would have taken endless time to unearth them. Yet as the red ants had seen their Chief and his friends almost drowned, they didn't want to leave without their revenge.

Their shouts had disturbed the pleasant slumbers of a dung beetle.

"Will you little pests quit making that noise?" he rumbled, moving out heavily from beneath a pile of rotten leaves. Slowly he lumbered toward the ants, turning his head from side to side and rolling his little blue eyes. His dark blue armor shone in the sun with a steely glitter. His enormous size, his thunderous voice, and the flash of his angry eyes would have frightened anybody. The beetle halted, seized the nearest robber, and wrung his neck with his strong hands.

"Now I'll teach you a lesson about making disturbances here," he said. "This is my property, and I'm in charge."

The robbers rushed to avenge their friend. The beetle seemed not the least bit afraid. With his two hands, one after another, he picked them up and tossed them away, dead.

But the robbers, in an endless stream, set on him so fiercely that he had to defend himself. Only one part of his body—his belly—was unprotected by armor. Knowing this, the robbers used every means

29

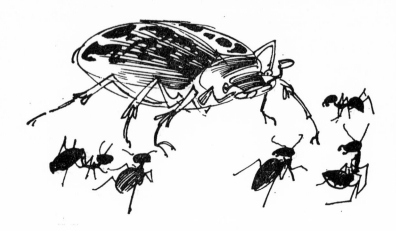

to get at that spot.

"Let's just see who'll win," mumbled the beetle, confused, as he pressed his belly to the ground.

"We'll see!" bellowed the furious robbers, digging the ground from under him. Soon they reached his belly and tickled it most painfully. The beetle stood up, to run for his life. At once the robbers attacked from every side, as they stung him from below. The beetle, exhausted and half unconscious from the poison stings, collapsed at last. Soon only his empty armor lay in a heap beside the brook.

The robbers reformed their ranks and, singing their war-songs, jauntily marched on through the woods.

5. THE ENEMY AT THE GATE

It was a radiant summer day, with only a few white clouds in the blue sky. The air was heavy with the smell of flowers. On such a day a lot can be accomplished, and the town of the black ants was hard at work.

The larvae and eggs, which were to become young ants, had been taken outdoors for the fresh air. The children, on top of the anthill, were in class. There they were studying the duties and ways of life in the ant community. Old Hustle-Bustle taught the girl ants how to work about the house.

31

At the main gate, laborers and soldiers were drag-ging in a dead earthworm. Hundreds of field hands were carrying into the town grains of wheat or grass-blades for house repairs. Anything useful from outside was being pushed or dragged home.

And the hunt was going well: several thousand little marauders, who had been hurting the plants, were being brought into the town. Some, the hungry workers ate on the spot; others were stored in warehouses for the coming winter.

Suddenly a worker appeared in the distance, running as fast as he could toward the town. He was so tired that he fell again and again on the road. Many others left their work in the fields and followed him in a swarm.

Near the gate they raised loud shouts of alarm:
"The robbers! The robbers!"

The consternation spread. The first reaction to this news was great fear. The workers, swarming in from every side, told of a great army of red ants drawing near. The enemy van had already seized some laborers in the fields.

The guards—old, experienced soldiers—shouted themselves hoarse from the walls:

"Take the larvae below! Hide the children in the cellars! Block the gates! Fill in that break by the road!"

Cries of alarm sounded in every nook and cranny of the town. The workers and soldiers rushed to save the larvae and eggs, taking them down to the subterranean chambers.

The Queens of the anthill, who numbered twenty-two in all, called an emergency council, which appointed a chief commander of the armed forces, approved a plan of defence, and issued the necessary orders.

At once the little emergency gate at the rear of the anthill, which opened on the underground passages and led to the foodstores, was blocked with sand. Companies were assigned to heighten the city walls and erect obstructions of every kind. Three detachments of young soldiers, untested in battle, were hidden behind the hill under the leaves of a wild strawberry, as a reserve to be brought in as the need arose.

The strongest force was sent out to meet the enemy before the main gate and to inflict on him a decisive blow. Others were stationed inside, to be ready if the enemy breached the wall.

After the first wave of panic, the town fell silent. Every soldier knew his post, every worker his task; the leaders did not need to rush to give instructions, nor to answer questions.

Calm and determined, the troops crouched close

to the sacred soil of their town, which was a part
of themselves. They understood what sacrifices
were expected of them.

In the distance, on the great road, which had
only recently been repaved, the first detachment
of the robber army appeared. Even from afar, their
grim faces and raised swords could be clearly seen.

6. THE BATTLE

The robbers halted before the main gate of the town. Following the orders hoarsely shouted by their officers, they separated into detachments and took up battle positions. Iron Jaw stepped out ahead of his army, climbed onto a tuft of moss, and addressed the citizens of the town.

"You all know well that our business is to rob and kill. Whoever opposes us, always regrets it. I offer you one choice: that between life and death. My personal advice to you is: choose to live. If this is your choice, open the gates now, and do

35

not resist. Otherwise, your town will become a graveyard!"

With these words, Iron Jaw so violently waved his claw that he almost toppled.

An uneasy silence followed.

Iron Jaw's speech was passed on to the Queens of the anthill. Even without their decision, the fate of the town was clear: not one citizen would have agreed to give his children into slavery, or to accept it himself. Indignation at the robbers' demands grew into real fury when the guards recognized the red ant who had abused the hospitality of the town, and who now stood beside Iron Jaw.

"Let's fight!" shouted the multitude in the main square. "We know how to defend our homes and honor!"

Only with difficulty could their officers restrain the soldiers.

The chief commander of the black ant forces, an old veteran of many battles, answered the robbers from the wall, in a curt tone:

"We choose to fight to the death!"

Then, turning to his soldiers, he added:

"Not a creature in the world refuses to defend its nest. From this moment, every black ant is a soldier. All of you know your duties."

As the commander finished, the whole anthill

shook with a battle cry. The soldiers poured out from the town, eager to fight and ready to meet death on the field. The robbers gave battle at once, and met the defenders head-on. A deadly struggle began.

A troop of black ants, led by a young officer, was the first to pierce the ranks of the robbers, and unexpectedly attacked Iron Jaw himself, where he stood surrounded by his aides and messengers, the traitorous red ant at his side. Seeing the enemy, the Leader drew his sword and rushed into battle. The young officer dodged his blow, turning instead to the red ant.

"Death to traitors!" he shouted, and seized the red ant so fiercely in his claws that both he and the spy went down. Clutching at each other, they rolled in the dust. The red ant managed to seize the officer's head with his claws, and tried to run him through with his sword. But the officer adroitly freed himself, jumped to his feet and, with one powerful stroke, ran the ant through, injecting a deadly poison into his heart.

The robbers rushed to rescue their Leader and his entourage. Soon the young officer and his detachment were surrounded. Ant grappled with ant, wallowing on the ground, rolling one over another, aiming their swords at one another's breast.

The example of the brave young officer so stirred his fellows, who had witnessed the scene, that they rushed into the fray troop after troop, trying to save the officer and his soldiers, who desperately held their ground. After a bitter fight, the black ants broke the encirclement, and the young officer, waving his sword, rejoined the main body. Although he had a large gash in his head, he stayed on the battlefield and fought with unabated fury.

The robbers, however, were far better armed than the black ants. One grip of their claws was so painful that even strong soldiers found it hard to bear. The robbers knew well the strength of their weapons, and relied on their skill to win the battle. And although they were meeting violent resistance, they had no thought of withdrawing.

Obstinately, the robbers penetrated closer and closer to the wall; then, with a great effort, they reached the emergency gate that led to the underground nurseries.

Near the gate, unluckily for the black ants, was a breach in the wall, made recently to drag in the earthworm. But here the robbers had to fight for every inch of ground, from one grass-blade to the next. Their thinned ranks pushed ahead, heedless of losses. The black ants stood their ground bravely. Here they were more numerous, several against each robber. Some would seize an enemy soldier by his legs, others by his hands, while others tried to inject a deadly burning venom into his wounds. The black ants showed real courage; even the wounded fought desperately with their broken weapons, or died without crying for help.

So many fell that there were several black corpses for every red one, yet they still resisted, and even attempted a counterattack with unimpaired bravery.

The dead and wounded lay in heaps everywhere around the wall, and the fight raged on.

Shrewd Iron Jaw saw at last that he could not win in open battle, and turned to a ruse. He began to retire with most of his army. The black ants, deceived, did not pursue him but concentrated against the force at the main gate. This was what Iron Jaw had counted on. He wheeled and rushed to the undefended rear gate, where, he knew from the scout's report, he would find the nurseries and foodstores. In a sudden, wild attack, he and his soldiers penetrated the town.

Within seconds, however, the reserve detachment, hidden nearby under the strawberry leaves, fell on Iron Jaw's troops. This new check stopped the invaders in their tracks and caused them enor-

mous losses—almost as great as those of the defenders.

Now the battle went on at every street-corner,
every door; wherever the robbers tried to advance,
the black soldiers refused to move from the spot.
The robbers gained ground over their own dead
bodies. The fiercest battle, however, raged at the
entrance to the nurseries and storehouses. The
troops were rushed from the main gate into this
last battle. You couldn't imagine the crush and the

uproar! Swords broke, the wounded cried out, the
robbers swore with anger and exhaustion.

Soon the red ants were surrounded. The Leader
saw clearly that he couldn't overcome the black
ants. At last he ordered all his troops to attack
the nurseries, break into them, snatch as many
eggs as they could, and then leave the town.

He himself, fighting with his soldiers, broke a
passage through the defenders and leaped down
into the underground passages. But in his haste

41

and excitement he lost his way, seeking the entrance to the nurseries in vain.

"Let's pull back, Iron Jaw," said one of his aides.

But he would not listen. He followed the dark, narrow corridor, hoping to hit on the way to the nurseries, or at least to find an exit. Here it was cool and damp, and his party found no one to guide them. Yet he rushed ahead, deeper and deeper into the anthill. At last the dark tunnel widened and branched into many passages, leading to other tunnels and caves. These were the winter quarters of the black ants, now musty, black, and uninhabited.

Seeing his mistake, Iron Jaw decided to go back. But then, by which way? There were hundreds of them.

"We're lost, Iron Jaw. And if we don't find our way out of these accursed caves, we're finished!"

Iron Jaw's eyes sparkled with rage in the darkness.

"An officer never panics, Lieutenant!"

Suddenly, with a tremendous crash, the walls began to collapse a few steps ahead of them. An avalanche of pebbles and a cloud of dust fell from above. The weight of so many soldiers, fighting above this particular spot, had caved in the pavement, half burying Iron Jaw in the loose sand.

"My Leader, are you alive?" shouted the aide.

"I am!" shot back Iron Jaw helplessly, though with contempt.

Meanwhile, above ground, the war had ended. The robbers had broken into the nurseries, snatched some eggs, and managed to lead away a few prisoners. Unable to hold out any longer, they hastily retreated. Among the prisoners was the old nurse Hustle-Bustle herself, whom the robbers had found in the nurseries. As they were about to kill her, a robber-officer named Brave Heart intervened.

"Killing old ladies won't cover you with glory, men! She can't even defend herself! Don't you see she's a nurse? Why, she's going to raise good healthy slaves for us!"

The robber army drew back from the anthill and halted behind the strawberries to wait for Iron Jaw. But he did not come back from the town. No one knew if he had been killed, wounded, or taken prisoner. But a few had seen him rush underground into the nurseries. And that had been the last of him.

The robbers had no time to lose, since the sun was low in the west, and they could not bivouac so near the enemy. The officers met and decided to march home without Iron Jaw. After the wounds of the injured had been tended, they formed ranks and set out on their journey into the woods. The prisoners and booty were placed in the center of the main column. As the red ants lifted their tired voices in the usual song of victory, it sounded almost like a parody:

Every foe comes to his grave
If he stands to block our will!
Coward, weakling, strong or brave,
All must lie beneath the hill!

Soon they entered the woods and headed for home, saddened by their defeat and the loss of brave Iron Jaw the Bad-Tempered. Many felt sure he had died in battle.

So many wounded and dead lay in heaps on the battlefield that the black ant townfolk spent the rest of the day gathering them up. They buried the dead and brought in the wounded. The ant doctors licked their wounds—it was the best medicine they had. The next day, the workers began to repair the town wall and the buildings. It was a long, hard task, but there was not time to complain. Every citizen knew that only his diligence and perseverance could make good the damage.

Yet there was one thing the black ants did not know. They never dreamed that deep under the town, in the underground winter quarters, the

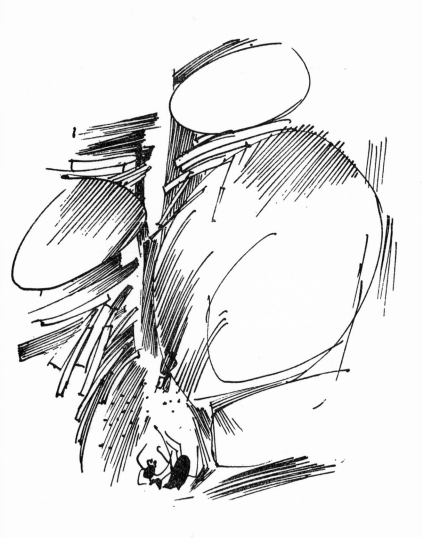

robber leader was trapped. There, unable to find
his way out, he shouted angrily and pounded on
the walls.

7. CAPTIVES OF THE RED ROBBERS

The army of the red ants re-entered their castle without the usual song of triumph. A small troop of soldiers, left to guard the quarters, met them at the gate. The returning warriors told of the fierce defense put up by the black ants, and of the disappearance of their leader. They delivered the booty, the eggs, and the prisoners, and scattered to their quarters to rest.

"What shall we do with the old lady?" sneered one robber, pointing at poor Hustle-Bustle, who was exhausted from the long march. "—Think I'll twist her head right off."

46

The old ant was indifferent to her fate and would, in fact, rather have died. Tears streamed down her face when she thought of her town.

"She seems to be a nurse. Maybe she could take care of the children," said another robber. "D'you know how to bring up the children, nurse?"

Hustle-Bustle nodded.

The guards led the prisoners into a deep cave under the castle. There it was dark, damp, and musty. The robbers locked them up, blocking the entrance with a solid pebble. As they left, one robber shouted to the prisoners:

"Don't think of trying to escape. That would be death!"

But none had the slightest wish to make such an attempt. Even if one managed to get out of the cave, how could he find his way back through the deep woods? The black ants often strayed far on long trips—two or three miles into the open fields —but they had no experience in woodmanship and knew none of the secrets of the underbrush and thickets. And if a slave did manage to run away, in no time the guards would capture him and kill him.

The prisoners were too wretched to think about such things. Old Hustle-Bustle couldn't close her eyes all night; her ears still rang with the shouts

of the black ant guards on the wall: "The robbers!
The robbers!"

This was no dream, but harsh reality. As soon
as the sun fell through the branches of the woods,
the prisoners were wakened by the raucous voices
of the overseers:

"Get up! Time for work!"

The stone was rolled back from the cave entrance, and the slaves were marched up to the
castle. The quarters of the robbers, filthy and
neglected, had to be cleaned and put in order. A
crumbling wall had to be repaired and leaky roofs
mended, before the rains.

One slave-gang was set to work on building and
house repairs, while others, mostly those born in
captivity, and reliable, were marched out to gather
food. The old nurse was led to the nursery in the
deepest underground cave, where the looted eggs
lay in disordered heaps.

"Care for them well," an overseer told her. "Be
sure all of them hatch. You must raise the young
as useful, obedient slaves."

Seeing the eggs from her native town, Hustle-
Bustle knew that the young black ants would never
learn of their own anthill, never see their brothers
and sisters, and work as slaves, all their lives.

With deep love and sympathy she touched them, she fondled them, and she set them in order.

One day, and another, passed. Like it or not, one had to get used to everything—to the strange, cold quarters and to the brutal, angry words. One who has always lived at home can never appreciate its comfort and warmth. Yet Hustle-Bustle forgot her sorrows, running upstairs and back down to the cave, taking the unborn ants for a sunbath on the roof.

A week went by, and the yellowish oblong eggs changed into little white creatures who needed ever more attention and care. With love, and even more pity, the old nurse kept studying these helpless beings, licking them, and giving them their baths. In all this work she passed the days and nights of her captivity.

Gradually she accepted her new way of life, and even that of the robbers, to whom she felt thankful that she might care for the little ones.

As she rocked them to sleep, she sang songs about the homeland under the Big Fir and about the great, beautiful town so far away. But not one could understand, or speak. They had no eyes, no ears—they were but little wormlets who knew only the need to eat.

49

8. LITTLE ANT NIMBLEFOOT

One day as old Hustle-Bustle was working in the nursery, a wormlet began to let out a thin, elastic thread, which she twisted about herself, rolling within it until it covered her on every side. Then she fell asleep in her new silken bed, which veiled from all eyes the strange things about to happen.

The old nurse watched, her heart fluttering, sure that from this quiet larvae a beautiful ant would emerge. Night after night she kept watch, awaiting the moment when she must help the little ant break free from the silken bonds.

At last the moment came. Now it was no blind wormlet that moved inside—it was a fully developed, beautiful black ant girl, with eyes, ears, legs, and a pair of antennae—one who could hear, see, talk, and run everywhere.

With all her strength she tore at the swathings, for her first breath of air. At the same time, she sensed that someone was tearing at her smothering cage, to help her. Then, all over her, a cool, refreshing draft bathed her. When the impatient little ant was about to spring from the cradle, she heard a voice:

"Wait, let me help."

But the little ant was already on the floor when she understood the nurse's words.

"My goodness, you are nimble!" said the old nurse, as the new ant ran everywhere in the nursery, looking at everything she saw, touching every object with her long "feelers," or antennae.

"What's this?" she asked, studying the other larvae.

"Wait!" said the nurse firmly. "Don't you know you've just been born?"

But the little ant ran and looked about, her eyes and mouth wide open, puzzled by all she saw and understanding nothing.

The nurse was amazed to see such a baby already so curious about all around her.

"Now girls like you should sleep and rest," she said, as the ant, when she had taken some food, once more set out on her rounds of the nursery. "I think, really, we should call you 'Nimblefoot'!"

Then the nurse made the bed and told the little one to lie down.

"Sleep first, and gain strength. Later I'll explain everything to you."

As Nimblefoot closed her eyes, the old nurse hummed an old ant lullaby to her:

> *Sleep sweetly on, my little friend*
> *Who cannot know the pains of labor.*
> *Too soon you'll work, and see no end*
> *As heavy toil becomes your neighbor!*

Gentle with hidden sorrow, the song lulled Nimblefoot to sleep. For a long time the nurse sat at the little bed, watching over the first child born to captivity. Nimblefoot slept soundly, and looked so beautiful that Hustle-Bustle couldn't turn her eyes away from the child's graceful, straight legs, her handsome, well-proportioned feelers, and slender waist. Looking at her closed eyes, the nurse felt love for this unlucky infant welling up in her heart. If only she could bear the hardships in store for this unhappy slave! . . . But misfortune had shackled the child, even in her cradle, and no one could help her support the weight of life.

Nimblefoot awoke, and the night was over. She felt stronger—she could run still faster! She was already on a tour of inspection when the nurse appeared.

"Well, Nimblefoot," said the nurse. "Who told you to get up?"

"I didn't want to sleep, nurse," said Nimblefoot.

"Come with me, then. I'll show you something."

Nimblefoot jumped up with joy. She wanted to see and know as much, and as soon, as she could.

The two of them went along a dark corridor, then upstairs, where a bright patch of light shone overhead. They climbed toward the light, and soon they were blinded by the radiance of the sun. The little ant staggered in the fresh, warm air, the pure white sunlight, and the blue expanses of sky. She felt as if someone were stroking her cheeks, softly and with infinite kindness. Full of contentment, she clutched the hand of the old nurse.

"What is that softness on my cheeks?"

Hustle-Bustle smiled.

"It's the wind, little Nimblefoot, the wind that flies with no wings down the blue sky."

Nimblefoot was dazzled, seeing the world for the first time. The sun shone, the trees rustled, the

53

wildflowers swayed in the wind, and the juniper-bush by the castle was all covered with greenery. It was so easy to breathe out here, and warm, and lovely, that at first she didn't know where to look, or what to say or do.

"And what's that bright yellow circle up there?"

"It's the sun."

"And what is the sun?"

"The sun is the mother of all the animals and plants. Without her bright rays, nothing could thrive on earth. They give us strength and joy."

"And what's this over here? What's that over there?" kept asking Nimblefoot, pointing all around with her little leg and oh'ing and ah'ing with surprise.

The shrubs and multi-colored flowers drew her as if they called her name, inviting her to go with them to far places deep in the woods, where, she thought, everything must be new, marvelous, and beautiful.

"How wonderful the world is!" cried Nimble-foot. "How tall the trees are—how high the sky!"

The old nurse patiently answered all the little ant's questions and added her own remarks and instructions.

"Enough for today," she said at last, and led Nimblefoot by the leg back down to the nursery.

There below, the darkness and the damp, musty walls made Nimblefoot feel forlorn. But she didn't have the heart to tell the nurse, and went obediently to bed. Then the nurse spoke to her of the sky and the sun, the flowers and the woods, and about life that was so full of marvelous things. The little ant listened without a word. The nurse talked far into the night, but she didn't say a word about the robbers, or the slave's fate in store for Nimblefoot. The burdens of life could wait, while Nimblefoot enjoyed the lullabies, the fairy tales, and the love of the old nurse.

9. THE LITTLE SLAVE

Soon Nimblefoot became a real ant, strong and quick, and she learned to help the nurse in her work.

One late afternoon Hustle-Bustle came down to the nursery and sat down by Nimblefoot. That day, she felt weary; the young ants had begun popping out of their larvae one after another, and all had to be helped out, and fed, and cared for. But she didn't love any of them half so much as she loved Nimblefoot.

Unexpectedly, a robber came down into the nursery. He looked unlike any ant Nimblefoot had imagined in her life. He was all red, his face was grim, and his eyes had an angry look. His pair of claws was huge and dreadfully sharp. Terrified, Nimblefoot trembled and huddled closer to the nurse.

"Hustle-Bustle, he scares me!"

The robber walked over and harshly asked Hustle-Bustle:

"Why are you sitting there doing nothing? And that ant of yours is big enough to go to work. What will become of us, if slaves learn to idle away their time?"

Muttering angrily under his nose, he turned and left, slamming the door.

"Why is that man so cross? Who is he?" asked Nimblefoot.

Like all who are young, she wanted to know everything at once.

The nurse saw she could no longer hide the truth. The time had come to tell Nimblefoot what she really was. She hugged the poor girl's shoulders and murmured:

"Nimblefoot, you aren't a child any longer. You're a full ten days old. Soon you'll be sixteen. What you hear from me now won't be a pleasant story. I'm not going to talk to you about the flowers and the beautiful world."

Nimblefoot saw deep sorrow in the eyes of the old nurse. She knew she would hear something very serious.

"My little child," began Hustle-Bustle in a shaky voice, "you weren't born in your own home. You won't even see it, ever. Your home lies far away, under a tall fir-tree, at the edge of the woods. But you'll never see that tree, nor the fields, nor the meadows that stretch far beyond the woods. You were kidnapped from your home. You weren't born, then, so you can't remember. The robbers, who assaulted your town, killed many of your brothers and sisters, and took you to make you grow up a slave. Now you must carry your burden in a foreign land—the burden of slavery. No one will pity you, no one will comfort you—you were born a slave, and a slave you must die. . . ."

"Nurse," said Nimblefoot, excited. "Let's run away—let's go home!"

"My baby!" cried the nurse. "What are you talking about? It would be a dangerous, impossible journey. Certainly you would die, from exposure or at the hands of enemies in the woods."

"But where is my home?" asked Nimblefoot.

Hustle-Bustle took her up to the roof and pointed to the west.

"There," she said, "where the sky is all bright with that reddish color."

Nimblefoot watched the sunset for a long time. The sun, half hidden by the trees, was crimson. It was as if a great fire burned there: a bonfire of joy, for whose warmth she began to yearn.

"Old nurse, I will run away! I must go home. And then I'll come back to get you."

"You don't know what you're talking about," smiled Hustle-Bustle. "First grow up, and get to know the world."

10. THE PLAN OF ESCAPE

As the sunny days of summer flew by, Nimble-foot grew, and became a serious, mature ant. Quickly she learned the necessary skills and was assigned to work at the robbers' quarters, where she could study their ways of life and learn many things about the life of a slave.

The castle, in the absence of a leader, was now ruled by the Council of Nobles, made up of the warriors who had been Iron Jaw's advisers. Nimble-foot knew them all, since she had to put their billets in order and bring in their meals.

All the nobles liked the young slave, who was cheerful, patient, and alert. No one had ever seen her sullen or sad. She had a kind word even for the dourest of the robbers, and she always consoled the other slaves who shared her fate. Nimblefoot never complained and never felt dispirited after a day of hard work, when she came back late to the slaves' quarters. And she never told anyone of her hope to escape.

One of the robber warriors was especially courteous to Nimblefoot. He always talked in a gentle tone and spoke many a friendly word to her. He was Brave Heart, a high officer and a kind person, though somewhat haughty and inclined to boast. It had been through his influence that Hustle-Bustle was spared during the assault on the nurseries. He had received his name for distinguishing himself in battle. Once, surrounded, he had fought single-handed, had cut himself out of the encirclement without help, and had, at the same time, rescued a wounded comrade.

Nimblefoot was horrified to hear him talk about wars, battles, and massacres. She would never have harmed any living creature: she knew that every living thing, however small or weak, wants to live and tries to protect his life. But Brave Heart loved to speak of his military exploits. Whenever Nimblefoot brought him his meals, he would describe his many wounds and show her his scars, telling in detail how and when he had gotten them.

Nimblefoot soon felt in her tenderness that Brave Heart loved her. This he never told her, but Nimblefoot could see it in his glance and his courtesy. But she had no wish to be loved by a robber. She began to avoid Brave Heart; she even asked her slave friends to carry his food and clean his room, taking over their harder tasks herself. Yet Brave Heart remained pleasant when he happened to meet her; he made her talk, and spoke to her in a kind, respectful way.

Nothing, however, concerned Nimblefoot so deeply as her secret thoughts of freedom. She yearned for nothing but her native country and her own town, of which Hustle-Bustle had told her so much. She had questioned the nurse in detail about her people, and everything at home. An ever-increasing longing drew her to them. Finally she decided she would run away, whatever the obstacles. Of what value was the life of a slave? Nimblefoot felt that death itself was worth far more, if it came through the effort to be free.

When Hustle-Bustle first heard of this, she didn't know what to think, much less what to advise.

"Is that a deliberate decision, Nimblefoot?" she asked in a shaking voice.

"Yes, nurse," answered Nimblefoot. "I will not remain a slave any longer. I must go find my home. I'm leaving this very night."

"It might be the best thing you could do," said the nurse. "But can you even guess all the dangers and hardships ahead?"

"I've thought of everything," answered Nimble-foot firmly, "and I'm not afraid."

The old nurse thought for a while.

"All right," she said at last. "I should be glad I brought you up to be so brave."

Then Hustle-Bustle took Nimblefoot aside, made her sit down, and began to tell her of all the dangers she would probably meet on her journey. First of all, Hustle-Bustle advised her to be polite to every-one she met. If attacked, she must defend herself with her claws, scratching the enemy's skin and injecting into the wound her burning venom. Then the nurse listed in detail all the insect families an ant could rely on, and she warned repeatedly never to venture near the pit of an ant lion.

Night came, and darkness fell. The sky began to sparkle with bright little stars. The nurse went on talking to Nimblefoot. Then she embraced her and kissed her head, knowing she was saying good-bye to the one dearest to her in her wretched life.

11. THE ESCAPE

Nimblefoot had to leave the castle before sunrise, while the robbers were still sound asleep. The nurse spent the night by her bed. The girl slept calmly, unmindful of the dangers ahead. The nurse didn't take her eyes from the girl she was seeing for the last time; at dawn they would part forever.

At last, on the horizon, a thin streak of red appeared. The wind moved over the trees, and a flower near the window trembled and turned to the east. The clouds floating over the dim sky were edged with gold, and mist rose from the dewy earth into the still boughs.

The nurse wakened Nimblefoot.

"The sun will be up any moment, now."

Nimblefoot jumped briskly from bed, quickly washed her face, and packed some provisions into a pouch that nature provides all ants. She kissed her nurse for the last time and cautiously climbed toward the open air. Silence lay everywhere. The robbers slept on, as the world emerged from slumber.

Nimblefoot, walking as quietly as she could, came to the main gate. Now she had only to make a dash for the woods, where she could vanish into the shadows. But the gate was guarded day and night. She paused and listened. The guard was asleep on the ground by the stone wall—Nimble-foot heard his loud snores. As she sprang past him toward the dense ferns and dandelions, a few grains of sand rolled down the path and woke the guard.

"Hey! Who's there?" he challenged.

Nimblefoot shuddered with fear. She ran, but the guard overtook her at the very edge of the clearing.

"Halt!" he cried, and seized her with his rough hands. "Where do you think you're going so early?"

She made no reply, but stood numb with fear, thinking her life was at an end.

"Speak up! Were you trying to escape?" Then, getting no answer, he dragged Nimblefoot back within the gate.

"This little one has nerve! She knows the pen-alty. . . ."

He led Nimblefoot into the guardhouse and knocked on the door of the inner room.

"Officer of the guard! Officer of the guard, sir!"

The door opened and an officer's head appeared.

"What's happened?" he asked, angry at being wakened.

Nimblefoot recognized his voice; it was Brave Heart.

"I've caught a runaway slave, sir," said the guard. "She was already outside the gate."

Brave Heart stared at the escapee and, in his turn, recognized Nimblefoot. She felt his eyes on her, but was too embarrassed to lift her own.

"Did you try to run away?" coldly asked Brave Heart.

When she didn't answer, he said to the guard:

"You can go now. I'll question her."

Brave Heart led her into the underground guard room, at the roots of an aspen stump, one of which formed a wall. Little pebbles served as chairs, and there was a cot made of soft strands of moss.

Brave Heart sat down on a pebble and said to Nimblefoot:

"Sit down. Do you know the punishment given to runaway slaves?"

"Yes," she answered, defiant. "I know it."

"A terrible way to die, Nimblefoot. The hang-man will strangle you before the sun goes down."

"I'm not afraid to die," she said. "When I de-cided to try to escape, I thought of that."

Brave Heart said nothing. He got up and began pacing the room. Suddenly he turned and laid his hand on her shoulder.

"No—you cannot be killed! You must live; but you must also promise me you'll never again try to run away."

As Nimblefoot remained silent, Brave Heart lost his patience.

"Speak up! Do you want to live? Think what's in store for you!"

"I know," said Nimblefoot.

"Then you don't love me," said Brave Heart sadly.

"You are a robber," answered Nimblefoot.

Brave Heart winced. His eyes darkened, and he gave her a long searching look.

"Yes, I am a robber," he said slowly. "I was born a robber, and I must die a robber's death. But

I do love you. And your life is in my hands. I'm an honest robber, and I should have no mercy on a slave. But I do pity you! . . . Yet you can't love me. . . ."

"No," said Nimblefoot. "My heart may be little, but I know the worth of love and what death is. You must know, Brave Heart, that the slave is one who fears death. I won't be a slave. I'd rather give up my life, as any black ant is willing to do."

"All right, die, then!!" cried Brave Heart, his lips tightening. "Die if you want, and you shall, by sunrise!"

He paused, then he leaned over her.

"No, you must live. You are too good. Go in freedom and look for your home. Go, go, I'll lead you through the gate. And then I'll die—a traitor."

"No," said Nimblefoot. "I can't accept that sacrifice. Send me to the court, as you should."

He wouldn't listen to her.

"You must get out at once! Soon everyone will be up, and then you're lost! Come on, I'll take you past the guard. Come!"

He turned toward the door, but Nimblefoot didn't move. She could not see one who loved her die a traitor. But she was glad to see, even among the robbers, someone who could sacrifice himself for another.

69

"Brave Heart," said Nimblefoot, "you can do one thing for me without harm. Take care of my old nurse, and tell her I was glad to die for my country."

"I will," promised Brave Heart, turning away to hide his pain.

"And don't be offended, Brave Heart," said Nimblefoot. "You're the best of all the robbers; you have a gentle heart. But our lives point in opposite directions. Your happiness is in robbing —I find mine in sacrifice."

At that moment several robbers, who had heard of the capture, entered the guardhouse. They seized Nimblefoot, bound her hands and feet with a strong rope spun from a spider-web, and threw her into a dungeon.

12. AT THE STAKE

Nimblefoot lay on the ground in the dark cave. The sun was up. She heard the morning breeze in the leaves; bird songs rang in the woods. How lucky they were! thought Nimblefoot. They could come and go as they wished.

The robbers, too, were early risers. Already they waited impatiently for the slave to be taken to court and then to the place of execution in the public square. Everyone knew Nimblefoot, the most beautiful of the girl slaves, and all wanted to watch her suffer.

The court went into a short session. Nimblefoot was pale, and she could hardly stand. The robber judges expected her to cast herself on the ground at their feet and to plead tearfully for mercy. But she was silent and calm. She seemed indifferent to what was happening, and this drove the judges into a cold fury.

Nimblefoot didn't look at Brave Heart, who stood sadly at the far end of the courtroom, watching her.

An old, long-bearded judge, seated at the head of a table made of two square pebbles, addressed Nimblefoot harshly:

"Are you the slave who tried to run away this morning?"

"Yes," she replied courteously.

"But of course you failed!" smiled the judge maliciously.

"Yes, I was caught," admitted Nimblefoot in an unruffled tone.

The old judge frowned, his eyes popping out with surprise and indignation. He didn't understand how a slave could dare to answer in such a way.

"Enough!" he bellowed, jumping to his feet. "No further examination is needed. Her guilt is as clear as day. Secretary, write out the death sentence."

A lean, starved-looking robber bent over the table and began to write on a gnat's wing. It took him a long time to compose a proper sentence. At last he straightened, stood up, and read aloud what he had written.

"The Military Court of the Old Aspen Tree Stump, empowered to punish with death any inhabitant of the woods found in an act unpleasant to the robbers, has decided to punish the slave Nimblefoot with death by torture, for her attempt to flee the castle and to escape. The sentence to be carried out at once. Signed: Angry Beard, Noble President of the Court; Scratcher, Secretary of the Court; and Members of the Council of Nobles who rule the castle pending the election of a new Leader."

Cheers of approval and glee rose from the spectators.

"That's what happens to runaway slaves!" shouted the robbers. Two soldiers seized Nimblefoot and dragged her out. The sound of a gong, fashioned from the armor of an unlucky dung-beetle, announced the immediate execution.

The other slaves were forced to witness the death of their comrade. Surrounded by a strong guard, they shivered with fear. Old nurse Hustle-

Bustle had also been dragged to the square and stood leaning against a grass-blade.

A squad of soldiers then entered the square. Marching with a springy step, they led Nimble-foot to the stake. Her hands were bound, but her step was firm. Seeing her, the old nurse covered her eyes and wept.

The snare drums beat a tattoo, and the robbers formed ranks. Nimblefoot was tied to a hair-grass stalk—the stake. Her guards stepped back into the ranks. With her were now only three grim executioners, who were to torture her to death.

A ghastly silence followed, and Nimblefoot could hear the cheerful bird songs and the quiet rustle of leaves. The sun shone, the breeze blew as if nothing unusual were happening.

Nimblefoot lifted her head and looked at the woods for the last time. Then she turned her eyes to the west, toward her distant home, which she would never see.

Her thoughts were scattered by a short, sharp rasp of the drum, signalling the executioners to begin their bloody business; everyone who wanted to see the execution had now had plenty of time to arrive.

But just as the executioners approached, lifting their hands, there was an awesome happening in

the castle. Above the heads of the crowd a cloud
of dust shot up, and a large mass of loose earth

rose over the roofs like a waterspout, falling back in a rain of rocks onto the square. It swept away the stake, the executioners, and the nobles who were watching from the ramparts of the castle.

As it became known later, this cataclysm was caused by a hare who had been peacefully sleeping beneath a pine tree nearby. A cone fell and struck him so sharply on the tail that the poor animal leaped up in panic and dashed for his life through the bushes. But his forelegs caught in a juniper branch, and the hare didn't clear the aspen stump. One of his hindlegs hit part of the castle, and he ran on into the woods without a glance at the havoc he had created.

Most of the castle was now a shambles. With destruction and confusion on every side, the populace lost their heads. The robbers milled about in the ruins, grabbing each other by the beards, looking for enemies and finding none.

Nimblefoot lay half dead on the ground. The stake had fallen across her and was crushing her. Suddenly she sensed that someone had come to help her: the stake was pushed away, and someone was cutting the rope that bound her to it. Then she felt herself being lifted and carried away. It could only be one of the robbers, taking her back to prison. And then Nimblefoot lost consciousness.

76

13. FREEDOM

When she opened her eyes, Nimblefoot saw a little green bug sitting on a fern above her head, singing:

> *My heart, so full of the sun!*
> *Nothing is lacking for joy!*
> *For me, no dwelling spun*
> *Of gold or silver—none!*
> *My heart, so crowded with joy . . .*

Nimblefoot had no idea where she was. Certainly not in the robbers' castle—she was somewhere in the woods. But she couldn't see a living thing except for the green bug, whose monotonous song droned tunelessly on.

77

Suddenly a grass-blade moved, and Brave Heart came into the open.

"Awake already?" he cried with joy. "I was afraid, you were so lifeless. Now everything will turn out well."

The sight of any robber made Nimblefoot shudder with dread.

"Don't be afraid," said Brave Heart. "I'm the one who saved you. You're free now, Nimblefoot. You can go home."

"I may go?" Nimblefoot spoke with such unbounded joy that she herself became afraid. Wasn't it a crime any more to run away?

"Not so loud, little one," said Brave Heart, looking around. "We're near the castle. Though, with the confusion there. . ."

He ran up a fern stalk and looked toward the clearing.

"What a mess! It'll take them days to clean everything up!"

And Brave Heart told her what the hare had done. When the disaster struck, he said, he'd looked for her and found her under the stake. Unnoticed by his comrades, he'd carried her away from the clearing to a safe spot.

"Where's Hustle-Bustle?" asked Nimblefoot.

"She was looking for you, too, but I told her

to leave it to me. 'Take a robber's word of honor, everything will be all right,' I told her. She was so glad to see me with you in my arms that she couldn't find words to thank me."

Nimblefoot's eyes danced with joy. Now the path to her town lay wide open. Her hope to find her people shone forth again, brighter than before.

"Let's get away from here," said Brave Heart. "We can't stay any longer. I'll go with you and show you part of the way."

"Thank you, Brave Heart. I'll be grateful all my life." And she looked at him, her eyes full of appreciation. Her very heart was in her words.

Cautiously they left the neighborhood of the robbers' castle, passed under the bramble-bushes, and turned to a hidden track under the grass and moss, leading to the west.

"Follow this path," said Brave Heart, "and you'll find your home. Walk toward where the sun turns red in the evening. Don't hurry; doing something very important, one must take time to think. If you get in trouble, don't lose your head. My grandfather used to tell me: 'If danger doesn't scare you, you'll frighten danger.'—And keep your eyes on the sun and the trees."

Thus Brave Heart instructed Nimblefoot as he led her through the woods. At last he stopped, looked at the sun, and said after a short silence:

"Good luck, Nimblefoot—and find your home. I do hope to see you again! And do you know how? You'll come back for your old nurse. I must tell you something really important, Nimblefoot. During the last war with your town, our Leader, Iron Jaw, lost his way in the nurseries underground. I saw the earth cave in and obstruct the exit. Tell your people to look for him; if they find Iron Jaw still alive, they can exchange him for Hustle-Bustle. But let it be your own idea, not mine. No one must know I told you this. There are some things we aren't supposed to tell anybody."

"Thank you, Brave Heart," said Nimblefoot. "Now my journey will have still another goal. Goodbye, goodbye."

She offered him one of her feelers, which the ants use as hands.

"Don't worry about your old nurse, Nimblefoot," said Brave Heart. "I'll have her assigned to take care of my quarters, and I'll do all I can to make her old days happier."

"Brave Heart, you're a true knight," said Nimblefoot.

Suddenly she embraced the robber and kissed him. His eyes welled full of tears. Brave Heart looked both happy and sad. He gave Nimblefoot a military salute and said:

80

"We must sacrifice much for others. And that's heroism, isn't it?"

"Of course," said Nimblefoot. "Now I know a robber, too, can be a hero."

Brave Heart said nothing more. He smiled, looked at her for the last time, turned sharply, and walked away at his soldierly pace.

Nimblefoot was alone in the center of the great woods. Tall trees swayed and sighed above her head, shadows swept back and forth under their moving branches, and calls, whispers, and rustlings stirred all about her. But she wasted no time gaping at the wonders of the woods.

At once she set out along the narrow trail that meandered amidst the grasses and shrubs. It was hard going. She had to climb over fallen grass-blades and dry leaves lying across her path. Yet, despite every difficulty, Nimblefoot stepped along briskly, her heart so joyous that she would gladly have suffered twice as much to get home.

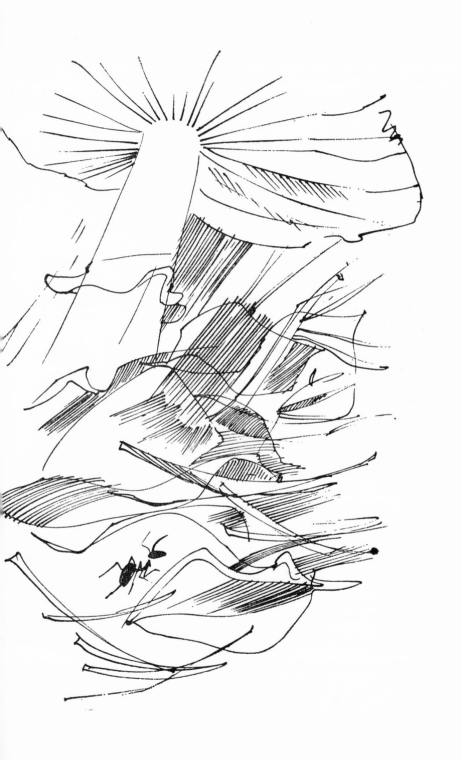

Toward evening she met an ant, black like herself, but of a different family, and she spoke to her.

"I've run away from the robbers' castle, and now I'm going home. My anthill is supposed to lie at the edge of the woods, under a big fir-tree. Do you know if I'm on the right path?"

The ant thought for a while, then said:

"Yes, I've heard of your town, but I don't know exactly where it is. Is there any other way I can help you?

"No, thanks," answered Nimblefoot.

"Why don't you come with me to our town? You'd get something to eat there, and a bed to rest in. It's not far from here."

"Thanks, I'd rather not," said Nimblefoot again. "I'd like to see your town, but I'm in a hurry to get home. Is your town like mine?"

"I shouldn't think so," answered the ant. "We're gardeners, you know. This spring we've already planted large tracts with vegetables, and they're sprouting already. What a lot of work, and so much worry! Just imagine, last year a frog trampled down more than half our crops!"

Nimblefoot had heard much about the ant gardeners, who had large farms and grew a vegetable called "the spore." They cared for the plants, and

84

for wintertime prepared a tasty food from their produce. Though she was curious to see their gardens, she decided that, above all, she must not leave her path. Nimblefoot thanked the ant for her invitation and accepted some food from her.

"Good luck," said the ant, and ran along her way.

Evening came. Nimblefoot stopped for a little rest and for a look at her surroundings. The sun had set beyond the woods. Now the big disk of the moon was already glittering above the treetops, and its bluish light made the dewdrops sparkle like silver. Still higher, the stars shone, gazing down kindly upon the earth, as if curious to know the secrets of these wide, dark woods.

Exhausted by all she had gone through, Nimblefoot paused to take in the beautiful sights of the night. She didn't feel sleepy yet, and she couldn't get used to the idea of her new freedom.

The sad song of a night insect reached her ears. As she listened, she could hear thousands of other voices from the mosses and grasses, from high in the branches of the trees, and from the shadows of the bushes. All these voices melted together into one harmonious sound—quiet, happy, and peaceful—which streamed over the ground and vanished into the depths of the woods.

"So, many creatures stay awake at night," mused Nimblefoot, surprised. And then she recalled the words of Hustle-Bustle, which the old nurse often repeated to every generation of young ants: "Life is beautiful and full of wonderful things, but it is short. We shouldn't waste a minute of it."

Nimblefoot got up and set forth again.

It was past midnight when, all tired out, she had to stop for another rest. A wild flower was growing by the trail. Nimblefoot decided to spend the night in its blossom. She climbed the slender stem and knocked on the calyx.

"Who is it?" asked the flower in a soft voice.

Nimblefoot told who she was. The blossom opened cautiously, and a white face looked at her with suspicion.

"What do you want, so late at night?"

"Please, let me sleep here," said Nimblefoot. "I'm very tired, and I need rest."

"Come in," said the flower at last. "Only, please be careful. Don't waken the ones who're already asleep."

Nimblefoot looked inside and saw two little red bugs, sound asleep in the center of the blossom. Hand in hand, they huddled close to each other like two little brothers. Nimblefoot wanted to ask

them who they were, but she remembered her
promise. Carefully she stepped inside, lay down,
and fell into a deep sleep.

15. IN THE WILD CRICKET'S CABIN

When Nimblefoot awoke, the sun was already up. Its warm rays were caressing the trees and flowers, and the air was full of insect-voices. A crowd hummed and buzzed on the flowers and shrubs in a little clearing nearby. Many creatures Nimblefoot had never seen or heard about. Swarming into the woods, they flew past with loud greetings and disappeared in the sunlight, which shone like dust of gold.

Nimblefoot thanked the flower for its hospitality, and slid down its stem. She found her old path and raced on as she had done yesterday.

At times the sun seemed hidden behind clouds, so dark and heavy were the shadows of moss along the trail. But soon Nimblefoot reached a series of little clearings and meadows, in whose fresh greenery, on blossoms, butterflies and beetles sunned themselves, half dazed by the fragrance.

Everywhere she could see myriads of little citizens of the woods—in hollow trees, in cracks in the ground, and under the leaves of past years. But Nimblefoot had no time to stop and look or speak. Here she felt like a stranger. And of course, it wasn't for her to meddle in other people's affairs. She was in too much haste even to sample the sweet elixir of the flowers, which the bugs were gulping down.

When night again drew near, Nimblefoot had covered a good stretch of the way. But she felt afraid that in her haste she might have lost her path. That would be easy here in the woods, with trails crisscrossing in every direction and travelled by all kinds of creatures, some panting under heavy burdens, others swiftly running along.

And now it was time to look for some refuge for the coming night. Suddenly, in the depths of the woods, she heard a song unlike any she had ever known before. The song was so tuneful that she paused to listen. Then she felt a desire to see

the singer. She went closer to the brookside, from which the song seemed to come.

In the bluish moonlight filtering through the grass she could see a little cabin with a strange fellow standing on the doorstep, a fiddle in his hands. His jacket was dark brown, tight-fitting and cut like a military tunic. He had three pairs of legs, of which the hindmost were enormously long. He stood there, motionless and dejected, his head bowed low.

The strings will sing, tri, tri, tri!
The clear notes of my song
Will echo far and long
To one who'll think of me, tri, tri, tri.

Flow, my song, flow, ta, ta, ta,
Full of my fondest dreams!
For you my longing streams,
Longing and singing, ta, ta, ta.

For I await you, tik, tik, tik.
Dear love, don't fall asleep!
I, alone in the deep
Woodland. . . Come soon or late, tik, tik, tik.

Then he stopped and leaned on his fiddle, deep in his thoughts. Nimblefoot liked the song, though she couldn't grasp what it was about. She wanted to talk to the player, but she felt shy before such an artist. Yet he looked so pitiable that she gathered her courage and walked over to him.

"Forgive me, sir, I wanted to tell you—I've never heard a song as beautiful as yours."

The stranger moved his forelegs and pointed them directly at Nimblefoot. Seeing that this took her aback, the musician hastened to explain.

"Obviously, little one, you've never seen a wild cricket, since you don't even know that he hears with his forelegs."

Nimblefoot found this most strange.

"But if you liked my song, I can repeat it."

And without further ado he lifted his fiddle and played the song again. Nimblefoot could now clearly see his instrument. It was a simple one: the cricket had two pairs of wings, the upper pair of which was narrower and shorter than the one beneath; with these he was playing, as he scraped the left wing over the right. Nimblefoot listened enchanted to his wistful music.

"Sir, what is it you want so much?"

"Well, I'm longing for the one I've so often dreamed about. We crickets can love only once in our lives. And love is the greatest thing life can offer. I sing to call to my beloved—she can't sing, herself. She'll hear my song, come to me, and become my wife. And we'll live only one day together—the day of the wedding. Then I must die."

"Die?" asked Nimblefoot, shocked. "What
makes you think so?"

He smiled, as if to him the idea of death were
not at all terrible.

"She'll have to die, too, as soon as the eggs are
laid. We crickets die at once after our wedding.
That's our fate."

Nimblefoot couldn't follow him very well, and
what she thought she understood she didn't believe.

"Please, come on in," said the cricket to Nimblefoot. "You look tired. Come in and spend the night
in my cabin. It's empty, anyway. I only sleep during the day."

Nimblefoot thanked him and went inside. When
the cricket came in to make light, Nimblefoot told
him of her escape from the robbers and her wish
to find her home town. The cricket listened, fascinated; then he said:

"I admire your courage! I've heard many things
about the ants and bees. Those insects are the
wisest and most respected of all."

Nimblefoot was too modest to say anything.

"You can go to bed now," said the cricket.
"Now I must go out and play till dawn."

He went outdoors and again began to fiddle.

Nimblefoot lay down on a bed of moss and fell asleep, lulled by the cricket's songs, which mingled with her dreams.

It was already dawn when the song abruptly ended, waking Nimblefoot with a start. She heard someone talking outside the open door in a gentle voice. Then she recognized the voice of the cricket, answering tenderly.

"I'm glad!" the cricket was saying. "You heard my call and you came. I've waited a long time."

The cricket came in, followed by a beautiful lady who looked much like himself. The cricket introduced her to Nimblefoot:

"This is my bride. Our wedding will take place today, at sunset."

"Sunset is the most beautiful part of the day, isn't it?" she said to Nimblefoot.

When the cricket's bride turned around, Nimblefoot saw a sword at her side. Yet the cricket was entirely unarmed. Nimblefoot was curious to learn why a young lady should carry arms; but she felt too shy to ask. And she felt she shouldn't disturb the young couple. As she was about to leave, the cricket stopped her.

"Why are you in such a hurry?" he asked cordially. "Stay with us today. For you to join our wedding feast would be a great honor, both to my bride and myself. I'll introduce you to the other guests—there'll be many there, and some might know about your town—it may be, they could even give you directions."

His bride, too, begged Nimblefoot to stay.

"Don't deny us that pleasure," she said. "I want so much for you to see our wedding!"

At last Nimblefoot gave in. But as soon as she was alone with the cricket's bride, she asked her:

"Please forgive my question, but why do you carry a sword?"

"It helps me hide the eggs under the ground," casually explained the future Mrs. Cricket.

16. THE CRICKET'S WEDDING FEAST

Endless preparations for the banquet were soon in full swing. Neighbors and friends, attracted by the bustle, kept dropping in, and they graciously accepted the invitation to stay. They had to be entertained and given food and drink. All this was further complicated by the guests' differences of diet and taste. The cricket, eager to please everybody, insisted upon serving each one his favorite dish.

His bride went out to gather sugary larvae from the shrubs and juicy earthworms from beneath the mosses. These she carried to the cabin and set on the table covered with white petals of camomile. At last all difficulties were overcome, and long before sunset the table was groaning under many kinds of meats.

There were fat worms, white, green, and brown; soft, tender young earthworms, which kept squirming in a vain hope to escape; an appetizing choice of flies, the favorite dish of the cricket's neighbor, Mr. Spider; fresh larvae to make one's mouth water; and all kinds of light snacks—gnats, and aphids, which the ingenious cricket had himself collected for this feast of his last, short-lived happiness.

Everyone's eyes, however, were drawn by a large keg, made of the shell of a filbert nut, filled to the brim with foaming beer flavored with fragrant roots. The bride had brewed the beer from a barley-grain the cricket had bought, after long bargaining with old Mrs. Sparrow, for a few seeds of hemp. He had saved it for just this occasion.

And even this was not all. In the center of the table stood a large cake. It was a crumb of bread, dropped by shepherds lunching in the woods, which the cricket had kept hidden in his cabin for a long time.

When everything was ready, the cricket and his

bride served their guests. Nimblefoot, who had helped with the preparations and the house-cleaning, was now asked to carve. Revolted as she was by the look of some of the dishes and by what went on in them—especially by the struggling earthworms—she didn't have the heart to refuse.

As soon as the sun had set behind the trees, the guests swarmed over the cabin. First to arrive were the relatives of the bride and groom: several young crickets, who had brought along their fiddles to en-tertain the guests. Other distinguished guests were: a bug in violet-colored armor, who called him-

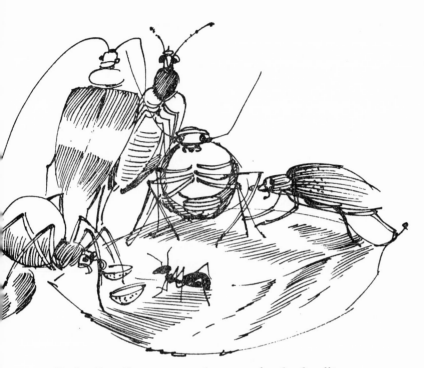

self the Jeweller, a great boaster, fond of telling
tall tales; a nutbug, who looked comical because
of his enormous nose—with its tip he nibbled at
everything in reach; the bark-beetle, who lived in
a pine-tree nearby; a ladybug, the Poetess, who
was asked to recite some verses for the occasion;
the inhabitant of a distant swamp, a waterbug who
loved to swim on his back; and Mr. Spider, who
tended his nets not far from the cabin.

There was also the Pharmacist, Fir-Tree-Bug,
proud and pompous, his hair receding at the
temples because of his wisdom and his alleged

knowledge of Latin. His other distinctive trait was an enormous pair of whiskers, longer than his entire body. He walked with them thrown back over his shoulders.

The Mushroom-eater was conspicuous for his bright red head (which, however, contained little wisdom), and for a pair of red trousers.

Peace and order were entrusted to the green-uniformed policemen of the meadows, who were armed with real rifles.

Nimblefoot shuddered with fright when she first glimpsed the Prophet of Death, a tall black beetle, who sat motionless and unsmiling. But he was of a kind, good-humored disposition. Only superstitious human beings had given him his gruesome name.

The company was both lively and polite. Everybody talked, made jokes, and laughed a lot. Only the rosebug held himself somewhat aloof. He lived on the rose-bushes, and that's probably why he looked down his nose at the other guests and talked of nothing but rose nectar.

The cricket kept running back and forth around the table, helping the conversation among the guests.

"Please, everybody, help yourselves to anything you like, and take as much as you can put away."

100

At last he found time to sit down beside his bride at the head of the table. To his left sat the haughty rosebug, and on the other side, next to the bride, sat Nimblefoot. Opposite her, the cockchafer was making everybody laugh with his funny stories. He kept teasing the bark-beetle, saying that Mr. Woodpecker would punish him for spoiling the bark of the trees. The poor bark-beetle trembled with fear at the least mention of Mr. Woodpecker. He was growing angry, and begged the cockchafer to stop. But this only inspired the latter to further fooleries.

"You may be sure, dear bark-beetle, that when you get home you'll hear Mr. Woodpecker knock-ing on your door, like this—knock, knock, knock!"

Everybody burst out laughing. Mr. Spider, gnawing at a fly drumstick, giggled, sighed, and said:

"Well, well, well ... Let's be merry, friends and neighbors, while we're here. But I wouldn't advise any of you to come near my nets tomorrow!"

"My goodness! Do you mean to say you'd do that even to me?" asked the ladybug, horrified. "To me, respetced by everybody, even human beings? Why, they say that if the woods are green, it's only thanks to me, because of the aphids I eat!"

"Why don't all of you stop this nonsense?"

asked the rosebug indignantly. "We didn't come here to fight; we came to celebrate."

"May I serve the ladies and gentlemen some beer?" asked the cricket, setting an overflowing jug on the table.

Nimblefoot sat quietly and ate little. She chatted mostly with the Poetess ladybug, who was talkative and knew many secrets of the woods and of their inhabitants. The two were soon close friends.

At the same time, Nimblefoot kept observing the guests, some of them friends, others enemies, though today all were in happy fellowship. She realized that Mr. Spider wouldn't let her go if she fell into his net tomorrow—but now he was quite friendly.

"Well, little one, are you having a good time?"

"Yes, thank you, Mr. Spider. And yourself?"

"Excellent, excellent! Just think of it—eating one's fill—and all free! The dishes are succulent, and the company outstanding. How often I've to sit in my net, alone for days on end, without catching a decent morsel! I wish the crickets would marry every day of the year! Then I'd sell my net and buy myself a tail-coat."

The guests talked as they ate, and when their hunger was satisfied, they drank and sang. It was fine to watch them when the table was almost bare,

and the keg of beer gone. Each one sang his own
tune, trying to drown out the others. They danced
as the cricket's relatives sawed on their fiddles, all
making so much noise (because of the beer) that
one wanted to stop his ears. The Poetess recited
her verses, composed for the occasion; the bark-
beetle sang a song praising the tasty pine-tree bark;
the rosebug sang of the fragrance of roses. Since
nobody would listen to him, the cockchafer kept
talking to himself. The cricket was in a jovial mood,
smiling to his bride and whispering endearments
into her ear.

"Sing, let me dance!" he shouted to the fiddlers.
"Cheer up these last hours of my life!"

The fiddlers began to play a square dance. All
the guests left their places at the table and swung
around to the rhythm, holding hands, scraping
their feet, and shouting with glee. The cockchafer
danced with the bark-beetle, so clumsily that you
couldn't help but laugh. Mr. Spider danced with

the ladybug. He swung his long legs around like a
windmill, hugging his partner, whose feet didn't
even touch the ground.

"Let me go!" she cried. "You're choking me!"

But Mr. Spider only laughed, whirling her still
faster in circles, paying no attention to the beat of
the music. Nimblefoot danced with the rosebug,
a considerate and courteous partner. If he stepped

on someone's foot, or bumped another couple, he never failed to apologize.

After this gay dance the sweating guests sat down to cool off. The cricket stood up and called for attention.

"I wish to thank everyone for coming to our wedding. My life is almost over. Please listen to my last song."

He picked up his fiddle and played as he sang:

> *I won't be fiddling any more.*
> *My joys are coming to their end.*
> *But you, dance on and on and on,*
> *Happy together, friend with friend.*
>
> *Alas! I can't sing longer now;*
> *I'll die before light fills the east.*
> *You, dearest guests, remain till dawn,*
> *Take joy together in the feast.*

Nimblefoot listened, perplexed, with no idea what he was singing about. She couldn't understand why the cricket sang such a mournful tune at his wedding feast. She hadn't believed him when he'd spoken last night of his imminent death. Yet, now it seemed true! The cricket and his wife bowed to the guests and left the cabin. In a moment Nimblefoot followed them.

"Goodbye, my dear," said Mrs. Cricket to her

husband, tenderly. "I'll die, too, as soon as I take care of the eggs."

And she slowly walked away into the woods. Nimblefoot, seeing the cricket standing motionless by the cabin door, asked him solicitously:

"Are you feeling ill? Can I help you?"

"No," said the cricket. "I feel fine, thanks."

And with these words he dropped dead to the ground.

Horrified, Nimblefoot fled to the cabin, shout- ing to the company:

"The cricket is dead! The cricket has just died!"

What was her amazement to see her words make no impression on the guests!

"Don't get excited, little one," calmly said Mr. Spider. "What's so unusual? Such is the crickets' life: they marry a wife, and they die."

The fiddlers played on as if nothing had hap- pened. The rosebug came over to Nimblefoot and said:

"I see you're still ignorant of nature's ways. You probably don't even know that many creatures live only one day! Should we be sad because that's their fate?"

He took Nimblefoot by the hand and led her to the center of the floor, where the guests danced with undiminished gaiety. But soon the merriment came to an end, in a very unexpected way.

A certain Mrs. Frog, an aged widow, lived at the brookside, near the cricket's cabin. She had come home late after a visit with her son-in-law and had gone to bed; but she couldn't sleep because of the noise the party guests were making. Losing her patience, Mrs. Frog got up and waddled over to see who was raising such an abominable racket.

So, at the highest pitch of the merrymaking, the door opened and a terrifying monster, with bulging eyes and an enormous head, lunged in. The very sight was enough to curdle the blood. The bark-beetle cried out and fainted right under the table. The musicians jumped out the windows, and the cockchafer crawled to Mrs. Frog on his knees, begging for mercy and kissing her hands. Nimble-foot, the Pharmacist, and the nutbug stood in a group, trembling with fear.

"Aha!" said Mrs. Frog, in a passion. "It's you, you roisterers! Don't you know it's already near dawn? Get out right now, all of you!"

Everyone scrambled away as fast as they could. And at once the cricket's cabin became empty and still.

17. THE STORM

Terrified by the monstrous appearance of Mrs. Frog, Nimblefoot headed straight for the woods, and ran at full speed as long as she had any breath left. She didn't stop to look or think where she was going. Already she was sorry she'd accepted the late cricket's invitation to the feast.

As the sun came up, Nimblefoot found herself in a part of the woods where nothing was familiar. Only now did she know she had lost her way. Luckily, she heard a voice nearby:

"Good morning, Nimblefoot! How do you feel after the banquet last night? That monstrous Mrs. Frog certainly spoiled everything. We could still have had a grand time. But of course one mustn't expect the impossible. We should be glad we saved our skins."

Nimblefoot turned and recognized a cricket who had fiddled at the feast. She was glad to see someone she knew.

But what was her surprise when, looking more closely at the cricket's head, she saw two diamonds glittering on his brow like stars. She hadn't noticed anything like that on any cricket's head last night.

"What is that, on your head?" asked Nimblefoot, curiously.

The cricket smiled in a painful way.

"Do you mean those two lumps I have this morning? They're a sign that there'll be a rainstorm soon. My head's already aching."

"That's strange," said Nimblefoot. "And when is the storm supposed to break out?"

"Soon. There'll be rain and thunder before sunset today."

The cricket was suffering severely; Nimblefoot could hear his teeth chattering.

"But you're going the wrong way, Nimblefoot," he said. "You're lost!"

"How can I find my way?" asked Nimblefoot hopefully.

"You must go to the right, then turn left, and then again to the right, and then again. . . No, I must go with you, at least part of the way."

She gratefully accepted the cricket's offer, though it did turn out to be quite impractical. An ant simply cannot keep up with a cricket. One leap, and he would soar out of sight. By the time Nimblefoot could reach him, the cricket was already tired of waiting. Finally they decided to part. The cricket gave her the directions as best he could; at the same time, he warned her:

"Don't travel all day today. Find yourself a shelter before it gets dark. Don't let the storm catch you out in the open."

The cricket's forecast came true earlier than Nimblefoot expected. As the sun left the zenith and leaned toward the west, the sky blackened and the air cooled. A strong wind arose, tormenting the trees, and raindrops began to fall. One hit Nimblefoot on the head, almost drowning her, and splashed her all over. She was as wet as if she'd been given a ducking. She made haste to look for a shelter.

But this wasn't so easy. Every living thing had crept into his hole, pulling the door shut behind

himself. Under every pebble and tuft of moss someone was already hiding from the rain.

Nimblefoot became almost panicky, as drop after drop flooded her up to the chin. Lightning flashed, and thunder rumbled all over the sky. But then she saw quite a comfortable spot under a young pine-tree, between its roots, where the wind could not penetrate and the rain did not reach. She crawled under the root and decided to wait for the weather to change. Even if she had to spend the night, the shelter was quite adequate.

Soon, however, Nimblefoot heard footsteps outside, and a muttering sound, as if someone were talking to himself. A brown beetle crawled into the room.

He was quite startled to see the ant.

"Now, what are you doing in my house?"

Nimblefoot had no idea the place was inhabited. It was an embarrassing situation. She apologized and explained that she was homeless. She had entered by mistake, being anxious to get out of the rain, she said.

As Nimblefoot was about to leave, the owner stopped her.

"Now, wait. Where can you go in this kind of weather? Don't think I begrudge you a shelter. Stay here till the clouds move on and the ground dries."

And in truth, it was no time to venture outdoors. The rustle of the rain had changed into a roar, and the water ran in streams down the trunk of the pine-tree, flooding the ground all around it.

So Nimblefoot stayed. To be polite, she started a conversation with the host. She told him about herself and her trip. The brown beetle listened with interest, and, when she had finished, he told her about himself.

"My name is Brown Sprinter. I belong to a family of famous athletes, all of them great runners. I ran in a contest at the stadium, just before we were rained out, and I took first prize—a big, fat leaf-worm."

"Congratulations!" said Nimblefoot. "And what a splendid prize!"

As they talked, they heard someone outside the door. In came a strange-looking fellow, all dripping with rain and carrying a mandolin slung over his shoulder. He looked like a cricket, except for the green color of his jacket.

"Good evening," he said courteously. "May I come in out of the rain?"

"You're entirely welcome, sir," said Brown Sprinter. "It would be sinful to drive you away in such weather."

"Well, yes, the weather is acting up, very much so," said the guest, making himself comfortable and leaning against the root of the pine. "I'd been invited to provide music for a gentleman's birthday celebration, and I stayed on this morning for an early lunch. As I was leaving, the downpour began, and now it's a horror to be outdoors."

"You're a musician, then?" asked Brown Sprinter. "What is your name, sir?"

"Why, don't you know me?" asked the guest in amazement. "My name is Mr. Grasshopper. I'm well known as an artist, everywhere in the woods. I happen to be a cousin of a friend of the uncle of a famous musician, a Mr. Cricket."

Nimblefoot told him of her recent acquaintance with the late Mr. Cricket and about his death. The story hadn't seemed to affect Mr. Grasshopper, really. Instead, he turned the conversation back to himself.

"When you plan your wedding, young lady, you won't be able to do without my music. I'll play for you with great pleasure, pay or no pay; enough, if you offer me a pitcher of beer or a cup of wine."

"Is that how you make your living, Mr. Grasshopper?"

"Quite so, young lady. And I receive so many calls that I almost can't keep up with them, running from dance to wedding, from wedding to dance. And I don't play to become rich—not at

116

all! It's simply that I can't live without playing.
I am an artist, young lady. I've been travelling
since last spring over all the woodland trails, a song
on my lips! And I'll go on till the cold hand of

autumn seizes my mandolin, and the wind says: 'That's enough now, Mr. Grasshopper.' "

After a short silence, Nimblefoot said:

"And I'm trying to find my home. You've travelled through all the woods and seen so much of the world, Mr. Grasshopper—did you ever happen to hear of the anthill under the Big Fir?"

"Yes, it seems to me I must have heard it mentioned somewhere, young lady," replied Mr. Grasshopper. "I have a vague idea it might be on the other side of the Big Lake. I've never ventured that far on my travels. But I doubt that a frail little ant like you, Miss, should undertake such a long, strenuous journey. Are you sure you have the strength to make it alone?"

"I'm sure," smiled Nimblefoot. "And I hope I'll succeed. Even if I have to try very hard."

Suddenly they saw a light outside, shimmering far away and moving toward the house.

"What could it be?" wondered Nimblefoot, peering out the window.

On the threshold appeared a little bug carrying a lantern with a greenish-yellow light, which helped him find his way in the dark. The bug seemed tired; he crawled his slow way forward.

"May I come in?" he asked at the door, uncertain whether or not to go away.

Brown Sprinter kindly asked him to step in. All
watched his lantern with amazement; as he crawled
in, the whole room became flooded with cold,
greenish light.

"Who are you, sir?" asked Nimblefoot, forgetting her manners in her curiosity.

"To tell the truth, I don't know myself which

of my names is the right one. Some call me the 'Little Dog of the Sun,' others, the 'Bug of Saint John,' though mostly I'm known as a glowworm," he explained self-consciously, placing his lantern on the floor as he sat down in a corner. Then he took something from beneath his jaw and placed it in his mouth, making a rubbing motion.

"What do you have there, sir?" asked Nimble-foot, fascinated.

"Why, it's only my toothbrush," answered the glowworm. "Pardon me, I always brush my teeth when I have a little spare time. I like to keep them white and shiny."

Now that there was light in the house, another guest turned up at once. It was a cockchafer, who walked in without so much as wiping his feet or saying a word of greeting. He made himself comfortable, and only then looked about him at the others.

"Aha!" he said in a hoarse voice. "I sure landed in good company. Glad of that. So much trouble in that rain! My helicopter engine stalled—wings got wet. A good thing I've several pairs of strong feet. Ran like a crazy centipede. In all that rain! You can get palpitations that way. My chest feels as if half a dozen ribs were broken," he rumbled on, pouring water out of his tall boots.

Middle-aged, the cockchafer was one who must have seen and experienced much. He took out his pipe, lit it at the lantern, and sent out a cloud of ill-smelling smoke, paying no attention to the others' comfort.

"Where were you going, Uncle?" asked the host.

"Delivering letters. I'm a messenger, y'know," he added to the strangers. "It got dark. What nasty weather, drat it! Maps wet, everything in a mess. Couldn't find my way. I, an experienced flier, to have to walk! It's a shame! . . ."

He mumbled on under his breath, as he puffed and blew cloud after cloud from his mouth and through his nose.

"Messenger duties are a real responsibility. One sends you here, another there. Always important! Births, weddings, deaths. Maybug's son-in-law swallowed by Mrs. Sparrow. Notify next of kin. On the go from dawn till dusk. I'm sixty now, thank God, but I've never been happy. What a life! Maybe when I retire. . . Were any of you at the meeting by the Big Lake?" he asked suddenly.

No one present had been there.

"I heard there was quite a crowd, though," said Brown Sprinter.

"Look here, now," said cockchafer hotly. "You,

brother, don't seem to give two hoots about politics. What's the matter with you, Sprinter? Are you on the side of the human beings? Watch yourself, fellow! You can be hauled into court for such ideas."

"What court?" asked Brown Sprinter, smiling good-naturedly.

"The Supreme Tribunal of the Frogs, buddy. The only court that can pass decisions on human acts. Haven't you heard the latest? What an atrocity! . . . They cut down the Old Willow Tree!"

"What willow tree?"

"The one at the edge of the meadows. They cut it down. Hundreds of cockchafer families homeless. Many widows, countless orphans. Terrible disaster!"

"But, who are the human beings?" shyly asked Nimblefoot.

"Look: another ignoramus! Where're you from, sister?" bellowed the cockchafer, pointing the stem of his pipe at her. He put it back into his mouth and bit it so hard that the stem cracked. "Shame on you, girl! Not to know what human beings are. . . Wait a minute, now, I'll explain. . . Well, the human beings are big. As tall as a tree. Four legs; but use two when they walk. Funniest of all, they think they're the kings of nature! Haw, haw, haw! I get a kick out of that, every time. . ."

"Then they aren't?" asked Nimblefoot.

"Who could believe it?"

"Preposterous!" added Brown Sprinter.

"The trouble is, they always want something they don't have. This, or that—whatever they happen to see. And right away, too. Can you think of a king wanting an old, rotten willow? They're beggars, that's what they are!"

"By the way, what was the resolution carried by the meeting?" asked Brown Sprinter.

"Well, the Chief Judge. . . You know, Mrs. Frog. A woman's a woman. . . Her speech made me cry. She said that they're about to let the water out of the Big Lake! She believes we must elect some other family of animals as kings of nature.— For example, earthworms. There are so many of them in the earth that in sheer weight they'd top the human beings, three to two! Voting on it next time. The earth belongs to us—insects, worms, bugs, beetles. Sure!" finished the cockchafer, again pulling at his pipe.

"Drat that tobacco: all wet!" he mumbled, standing up and walking to the door for a look at the sky. The rain had stopped. Far away, through the tangled branches, a patch of blue was already gleaming with sunshine. The blue spot widened, expanded, and split the black cloud in half. Sunlight flooded the woods. In it the light of the glow-worm's lantern could no longer be seen.

"Time to get going, I guess," said the cockchafer, pulling on his boots. "No one will bring my breakfast to me here."

"Is the world really as full of trouble as he said?" asked Nimblefoot, when the cockchafer had left.

"Well," said Mr. Grasshopper, who had been dozing at the end of the room. "I'm not sure I could answer that, young lady. Somehow, I think we find what we look for in the world, mostly. If we look for trouble, we get an armful of it. Myself, I look for happiness, and I do find lots of that, too."

And slinging his mandolin over his shoulder, with a gracious bow to the company, Mr. Grasshopper departed.

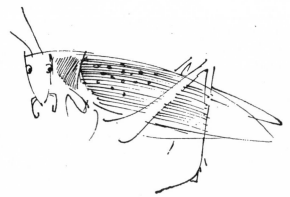

18. IN THE ANT LION PIT

Thanking her host for the shelter, Nimblefoot again set out on her journey. Unsure of the path, she wandered through the woods for the rest of the day. The hardly perceptible track she had been following was now almost totally covered by the rain.

Then she saw an old lady with a pair of horns, clinging to a tree trunk and, despite her strange position, calmly knitting away with a pair of long needles. Nimblefoot decided she must be a snail.

125

"Good afternoon, Madam," she said to the snail.
"Do you happen to know of the town of the black
ants, under the Big Fir? Being so high up, you may
have seen it in the distance."

"For heaven's sake!" cried the old lady. "How
could you have seen me up here? My gracious, you
must have eyes on top of your head!"

And she shook so much with laughter that she
nearly lost her grip on the tree.

"Of course I have eyes on top of my head,"
answered Nimblefoot, a little embarrassed. "And
I'm not joking, good lady. I have 123 eyes. Most
of them, 120, to be exact, can see distant objects

ahead of me, and the other three watch for things above and around me, at close range."

"So that's how you see everything so well!"

"That's true," answered Nimblefoot. "And every one of my eyes is really six smaller eyes! With them I can look in six different directions at the same time."

She felt too self-conscious, however, to continue this lecture on her own features. Just now she was more interested in something else.

"Well, you haven't heard of that anthill, then, have you?" she again asked courteously.

"To tell the truth, I'm not so sure," said Mrs. Snail, who wanted to go on with the conversation for the pleasure of talking. "In fact, I do recall having heard of it, some time or other. It's too bad I can't tell you exactly where, and how far, it could be. But may I know the reason why you're asking me about the location of your own town, you being a black ant? God forbid, did you get lost?"

Nimblefoot felt she was wasting time with the garrulous old lady, but she did feel obliged to answer her, and she told Mrs. Snail the story of her captivity and escape. It moved the old lady to tears.

"I sympathize so much with you, little one!" said Mrs. Snail with a suppressed sob. "It's too bad I can't help you. As you can see for yourself, I'm a poor, old, useless thing with my house on my back; I can't run about the district like a centipede."

"That's true, good lady! But thanks for your kindness."

"What's your name, my child?"

"Nimblefoot, Madam."

"You've been brought up very well, Nimblefoot. I'm really sorry I can't help you. It's been a pleasure talking to you. Have a nice trip, Nimble-foot!"

"Thank you, Madam," she said, and she left Mrs. Snail.

In a while Nimblefoot reached a dry, sandy spot amid a little clearing. Here the path narrowed and sloped sharply down. In her haste to make up the time she'd lost talking to Mrs. Snail, Nimblefoot didn't put her many eyes to good use. She saw herself on the brink of a funnel-shaped pit, but it was too late to stop. As soon as her forelegs touched the rim, the sand began to run from under her. Nimblefoot lost her balance, turned a somer-sault, and landed at the bottom of the pit.

The pit was narrow, and nothing was in it but sand. Yet as soon as Nimblefoot got up on her feet, a pair of strong hands emerged from the sand and seized her by the waist. Hard as iron, they squeezed Nimblefoot like a vice. In a panic, she struggled with all her might and managed to slip out of the deadly grip. Without a glance around, Nimblefoot scrambled up the steep wall, hoping to climb out. But the clever murderer, hidden under the sand at the bottom of the pit, began throwing handfuls of dust, to blind her. The sand ran from under her feet, and again Nimblefoot lost her balance. Once more she was at the bottom, but this time she knew what to watch for: the murderer whipped his arms in the air, attempting to seize Nimblefoot, but in vain; artfully, she was able to dodge them.

She knew she had fallen into the snare of an ant lion, the bitterest and most dangerous enemy of the ant family. Her life or death depended on a long struggle, and on sure calculations of every movement they both made.

Besides his powerful pair of hands, the murderer had a deadly venom which, but for Nimblefoot's speed, would have killed her at the start. Now she couldn't escape this vicious trap without outside help. No matter how long she dodged the murderer's grip, she couldn't climb out. Her efforts would only sap her strength, and then she would be lost. Nimblefoot began at once to shout in her loudest voice:

129

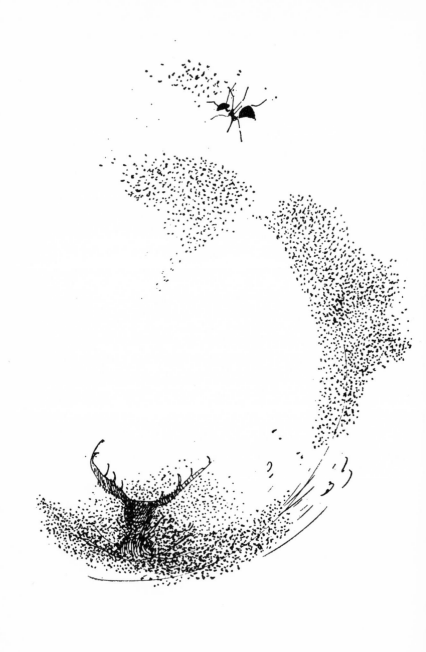

"Help! Help! I'm in the pit of an ant lion! Help!"

"No one can help you," sneered a low, hollow voice from beneath the sand. "This is your grave, my dear!"

And again he began throwing sand at her, so violently that it buried Nimblefoot almost up to her shoulders.

A shudder of cold fear shook her. Summoning her last strength, Nimblefoot crawled out of the sand, trying not to lose her courage and powers of judgment. She looked around the walls of the pit, seeking for some firm point. At one spot, about halfway to the top, a piece of gravel was sticking out. Was it strong enough to support her small, trembling body, at least for a while?

Nimblefoot hugged the wall and could feel the sand running all the while. She tried to move as cautiously as she could, but she made no progress. The murderer, meanwhile, was not standing idle. Seeing her scheme, he sent up a real hurricane of loose sand, blinding and choking her. He hoped she'd soon slide back to the bottom, exhausted. But Nimblefoot not only kept her grip on the wall; she even crept a little farther upward.

Finally the lion, as choked by the dust as his victim, paused for breath, and Nimblefoot swiftly took advantage of this fraction of a second. She jumped carefully toward the piece of gravel and reached it by a hair's breadth. She was lucky; the little stone held firm under her weight. Clinging to it with all her might, Nimblefoot caught her breath and looked down into the pit. The lion, seeing his mistake, leaped up in a vain attempt to reach her and to pull her down.

"Don't think you'll escape!" he bellowed at Nimblefoot's feet. "I'll toss your bones out of my pit, just like this sand!"

"Don't make promises you can't keep!" shot back Nimblefoot angrily, preparing for the first time in her life to use her own venom.

In a fair fight, she wouldn't have hesitated to challenge this little black wretch. He was underset, with a bulging belly. But of course Nimblefoot couldn't get at him in the sand, where he lurked with only his pincers and his poison needle visible. Yet she felt sure of victory.

The best thing to do now was to remain still and rest for a while. An attempt to jump out could be fatal, since she'd lose her grip and might again slide down with the sand into the murderer's pincers. The lion, too, found it wiser to lie in wait. He felt sure that the ant would be his, sooner or later.

Again Nimblefoot cried for help.

"Help me! It's Nimblefoot! I'm in the pit of an ant lion!"

A voice sounded in the distance, faint but very clear.

"Are you really Nimblefoot? Why didn't you say so right away, child? I heard you, but I didn't know who you were."

She recognized the voice of Mrs. Snail.

"Yes, Madam, I'm really Nimblefoot," she called back as loudly as she could, with new strength and hope.

Instead of an answer, she heard Mrs. Snail shouting at the top of her old, quivering voice:

"Everybody, help little ant Nimblefoot! She's in the pit of the ant lion! Everybody, help little ant Nimblefoot! She's in the pit of that wretched ant lion, in my neighborhood!"

And, for the benefit of Nimblefoot, she added:

"I'm coming too, with my whole house, my dear! Anyone faster than me, please help that poor little girl in the lion pit!"

"Here, here, I'm running like lightning," answered a husky man's voice from behind a dead tree-stump. It was music to Nimblefoot's ears. Her heart began thumping in her breast.

133

"Where are you, Nimblefoot?" roared the same voice at the very edge of the pit.

Well, he was none other than Brown Sprinter himself. Panting, with sweat streaming down his friendly face, he looked down at her and mopped his brow.

"Now, reach me that little hand of yours," he said, leaning over the rim. "Watch it, though. . . Easy does it. OK!" he laughed, as he lifted her easily out of the pit.

"Hey, hey, you there, what d'you think you're doing?" bellowed the murderer below, throwing sand at Brown Sprinter. "You thief! You've stolen my supper!"

At first Brown Sprinter paid no attention to him. But the ant lion became coarse and abusive and, in his rage, started throwing rocks at Brown Sprinter. At last Sprinter grew annoyed.

"Will you stop it?" he asked the lion.

But the murderer only heaped insult on abuse. Then Brown Sprinter picked up one of the larger rocks and flung it back into the pit. The shouting stopped at once. He looked down and shrugged his shoulders in apology.

"Can't be helped now. . . The fellow was asking for it. . ."

"I'm glad I could help you," said Brown Sprinter. "And by the way, just now I beat my own record!"

"I wish I could give you a prize for that," smiled Nimblefoot.

"Don't worry, this was no prize contest," answered Brown Sprinter, grinning from ear to ear.

Only now did Mrs. Snail, too, turn up. Covered with sweat, she called out from the distance:

"Nimblefoot, are you safe?"

"Yes, Madam, safe thanks to your help," answered Nimblefoot, waving her hand to Mrs. Snail. "How glad I am I met you!"

"I heard you when you called for help the first time, but I didn't know it was you. There've been so many cries around here lately that I just can't answer them all. Especially when one is an old lady with her house on her back. . . One can only help good friends."

Suddenly a buzz of wings was heard overhead, and a high feminine voice called down to them:

"Is that a funeral, or a celebration? What kind of verse shall I compose? Tell me, now!"

It was ladybug the Poetess: Nimblefoot recognized seven black dots on her upper wings.

"I would have come earlier, but I didn't know what kind of verses would be expected of me," said the Poetess. "I took time to compose two sets: one for a funeral, another for a safe escape. Which shall I recite?"

"Both," said Brown Sprinter.

"How's that?" asked ladybug, puzzled, and circling about like a whirligig.

"Quite simple," explained Brown Sprinter. "You'll have to recite one set at the pit, where a murderer lies dead, and the other here for Nimblefoot, who suffered no harm, don't you see?"

"I see, now!" said the ladybug, landing beside Nimblefoot.

As soon as she touched ground she recited some very well turned-out verses of congratulation. Then she walked to the pit, ready to begin her other set. But just as she struck a tragic pose, an awful roar in the sky made the air shake and the blades of grass bend down to the ground. A big plane dived from behind a juniper bush and hit a clump of moss with a loud crash, in a cloud of dust. Everyone rushed to the scene of the accident, expecting to find the plane dashed to pieces. What was their surprise when out of the pilot's cabin crawled the cockchafer, all smiles, and said laughingly:

"What a shame! Forgot to turn off the engine! Got a bruised nose, that's all. Say, how's Nimblefoot? The little ant, you know. Did she get away from the lion? Is she still alive?"

"Yes, she is—you can see for yourself."

"I'm too late, then. And I was in such a hurry. Congratulations!"

"Thanks," said Nimblefoot. "I didn't know I had so many good friends. I don't know how to thank all of you."

19. THE GRAVEDIGGERS

Nimblefoot felt sharp pains in her back and legs, and it was hard for her to move her head and antennae. The iron pincers of the ant lion had almost cut her in two. Luckily, she felt no broken bones. The fright, tension, fatigue, and her loss of strength began to tell on her.

She was too weak to go on with her journey; first she had to rest and recover. Slowly she walked to a little meadow, dry and soft with moss, and all fragrant with honey. Finding a comfortable spot beneath a wild clover, Nimblefoot sat down.

She felt thirsty, and looked around for something to drink. Nearby, on a leaf of wood-sorrel, a drop of dew sparkled, as pure as crystal. Her eyes brightened. She crawled to the leaf and drank deeply.

What if the lion poisoned me? flashed through her mind.

Nimblefoot stiffened with fright. She knew that the venom of an ant lion can be fatal. After all, escaping from his claws might not have saved her life!

"No, no," she cried, trying to calm herself, as she closely examined her hands and legs for telltale bruises. There was one on her arm, a slight one, doubtless received in the struggle. Carefully she licked it out, and then felt a little more relaxed.

All I need is rest, decided Nimblefoot, lying down beneath the clover leaves. She closed her eyes and fell asleep almost at once.

She was wakened by mournful singing in the distance. Chanted in chorus by many voices, the song had a strange, sad melody, unlike any she had ever heard. It sounded like a funeral dirge, or what she believed a dirge might be like—she had never heard one. The singing slowly came nearer from behind the juniper bush, and soon Nimblefoot could make out the words:

139

The days fly, they run and run,
The blossoms flower, then they fade.
Death comes to each and every one,
We vanish, with the tracks we made.

We soon forget the comrade gone
Whom we set in the ground today,
And none shall weep at his gravestone
For sufferings that on him lay.

We hurry now to shape his mound
And sing at his and others' graves.
By sacred duty we are bound
To tend the dead that nothing saves.

Nimblefoot lifted her head and saw a group of little insects with black-striped, yellow wings, marching in formation. They stepped briskly, and carried spades on their shoulders.

Are they coming to bury me? she wondered. Her hands went numb with fear, and she couldn't turn her eyes from the procession.

But the gravediggers passed on and stopped a little farther down, by a tuft of grass. The song ended, then, as Nimblefoot watched curiously, the gravediggers took their spades from their shoulders. Only then did she notice a black beetle in a glisten-

140

ing suit of armor, lying dead nearby. The grave-
diggers began to dig a hole right under the dead
beetle. They worked fast, the sweat trickling down
their faces. Every stroke of their spades was quick,
precise, and powerful. The corpse soon vanished
beneath the ground. They finished their work by
making a little mound over the grave, and then
stopped to sing the last stanza of the song.

Oh, let time darken sense and sight
Of one so still beneath the earth,
Who knows not sorrow nor delight,
But peace that was before his birth.

Nimblefoot felt sorrow grip her heart, and she wiped off a stray tear. Certainly this had been a real funeral, and a beautiful one. Who were those fellows who'd buried the beetle so impressively? And who could have hired them? As the grave-diggers passed her on their way back, one of them fell out of formation to adjust his spade, and Nimblefoot spoke to him.

"Thank you, sir," she said.

"For what?" asked the bug, surprised.

"For such a fine funeral."

"Why, we only did our duty, Miss."

"Do you mean to say you bury all the dead?" asked Nimblefoot.

"Certainly we do," answered the bug. "It's our business. That's how we make our living, and that's why everybody calls us the Burying Beetles, though, in fact, we are licensed morticians."

Nimblefoot took this chance to ask him whether he'd ever heard of her town. He said he had not.

"Too bad I can't help you, little ant. Though when you die we'll give you a truly high-class funeral. You can tell me right now where you'd like to be buried; then, later, there'll be no confusion. How about under this clover? Or would you rather lie under that wood-sorrel?"

Nimblefoot said nothing. The mortician, to brighten the gloom his words had produced, began to tell the story of the black beetle they had buried.

"He was a dung-beetle, and so no one loved him. One day he became friends with a girl—a glowworm. They would meet at night in the moonlight and ramble the woods together, he hunting, she lighting the way. One day she said to him: 'Is it true, you're a dung-beetle?' 'Yes,' he said. 'Then I can't be your friend. Forget me.' And she flew away, never to return."

"The dung-beetle mourned for a long time. He went on, sad and lonely, until one day he met a hornet. She was a proud, elegant lady, clad in splendid brocade. He had found her near his cabin, sick, wounded, and wet with rain. He carried her home and nursed her back to health. In her gratitude the hornet promised never to forget him. 'You saved my life, therefore you'll always live in my heart.' But these were only words. The next day, back from a visit to her native nest, she said: 'I'm very sorry. How could I know you were a dung-beetle? Why didn't you say so, right off? Thanks for your kind heart. Goodbye, and forget me.'"

"One day, again, he met a young butterfly named Fortuna. Seeing him sad and woebegone, she said to him: 'Why are you so melancholy in the middle of the summer? Come, let's be happy together.' 'Good!' he said. 'Now I can forget all I've suffered!' They met in a meadow where many flowers grew. There she'd sit and wait for him. He would try to learn to fly, and she'd laugh her head off."

"One morning, as he came to their usual place, he found her in low spirits. She sat on a camomile blossom, and didn't even look at him. 'Go, go away!' she cried. 'Everybody's laughing at me for keeping company with a dung-beetle. It was an honest mistake: I took you for a rosebug.' 'Yes, it's true—I am a dung-beetle,' he answered. 'But I do have a heart.' And that was true, too. But the butterfly flew away."

"He remained alone in the world. No one wanted to be with him. Then he came to this lonely spot, where he died broken-hearted."

As he finished his tale, the mortician shouldered his spade and ran on after his friends.

"Goodbye, ant! We have another client under the hazel-bush."

In a few minutes Nimblefoot again caught the distant strains of the funeral dirge, this time under the hazel-bush. She felt so touched by these sorrow-ful things that she could think only of her own certain death.

No, no, she still wanted to live, to find her home, to be part of the real life of her own com-munity. She didn't want to be buried deep in the woods, under a clump of sorrel. No, she must live —she must get home!

20. THE LADYBUG'S HELPING HAND

When Nimblefoot again woke, the short summer night had passed and dawn was at hand. But
she didn't feel a bit well. Her eyes didn't light
up at the bright gold sunlight on the silver drops
of dew; nor was she cheered by the buzzing of
the myriad insects on the blossoms, so glad to welcome the day. Heavy sorrow weighed down her
heart and sapped her strength. Listlessly, with no
interest in what she was doing, Nimblefoot found
a drop of dew and washed her face.

Oh, if only I don't fall ill, she thought anxiously, gazing at the rising sun.

"Good morning," said a familiar voice beside her. "Did you sleep well, Nimblefoot?"

It was ladybug the Poetess.

"I expected to find you here," she said.

"Oh, I'm so glad to see you!" cried Nimblefoot. "Thanks for not forgetting me. I feel sad today."

"Well, I said to myself this morning, why shouldn't I fly and see Nimblefoot? Today I have all the time I want. We can sit back and relax, and have us a real gossip!"

"I'm afraid I'm not at all well," said Nimblefoot. "After what happened yesterday, I may be suffering from a terrible illness!"

"And what illness is that?" asked the ladybug, horrified.

"I think it's the 'Sickness of Being Lost,'" replied Nimblefoot. "Many ants die of it. As soon as they know they've lost their way and are alone, their hope of ever finding their home dies, and they sicken and die, too."

"What are you talking about?" cried the ladybug. "You aren't alone! Think how many friends you have! Everybody loves you. And you'll certainly find your way home; just don't give up. I'll help you find it."

"Your words are more help than medicine," said Nimblefoot, brightening. "And who knows? Some day I may really get there. Now tell me the news of the woods."

"Well, the nutbugs have just had a new baby, and Mr. Nutbug has invited me to the christening."

"Is it a boy or a girl?"

"Why, it's seven boys!"

"Wait, I don't understand. Didn't you say *a new baby?*"

"My tongue must have slipped. Mr. and Mrs. Nutbug have had septuplets."

"Just think of it!"

"Yes, septuplets—seven babies at once! Both parents are overjoyed. Now he's flying all over the woods, inviting everybody to the christening party."

"Who'll be the godfather?"

"Why, the Admiral himself."

"And who's the Admiral?"

"He's a water beetle. He wears a blue velvet jacket with white stripes on the sleeves. And the godmother will be the wife of someone who lives only on linden-trees. And she has the most beautiful dress! It's dark green, with red trimmings along the edges. The nutbug would be glad to have you come, Nimblefoot."

"Do you think I should go?"

"Of course. Why not? You'll have a good time, and some guests may know of your anthill, too."

"All right then, I will," laughed Nimblefoot.

"We'll go together," said the ladybug. "And now, tell me what you think of the verses I've just made up for the occasion."

"Go ahead, I'm listening," said Nimblefoot, making herself comfortable on the grass.

"This time, they're in free verse—modern, you know," said the poetess. And she swallowed a few times, rolled her eyes, and then began:

> *Seven new kids,*
> *Yes, seven boys!*
> *The first will run, the second chase him,*
> *And the third catch them both!*
> *The fourth will be the naughtiest,*
> *And the fifth, the wisest:*
> *He'll dance with the sixth,*
> *While the seventh beats the drum.*
> *Mrs. Nutbug cooks nut porridge,*
> *Mr. Nutbug makes the cradles.*
> *And all seven frisk and gambol;*
> *The whole house will shake and tremble!*

"You'll make all the guests laugh!" said Nimblefoot with a giggle.

The ladybug was delighted.

"I put great value on your literary taste, Nimblefoot. And I know you're sincere. I can see why
everybody loves you—because of that."

Nimblefoot, pensive, gazed at the ladybug, then
shyly asked:

"May I ask you a favor, Poetess?"

"Of course, Nimblefoot."

"Since you can fly. . . . Would you mind looking
around a little for me? As I've told you, my town
is under the Big Fir. You might easily spot it from
the air. Would you do that for me, Poetess?"

"Certainly I will!" cried the ladybug. "And
what a good idea! Why didn't I think of it myself? Probably because we poets are so impractical. . ."

And like all true poets, being impulsive as well,
she opened her wings at once.

It was a long while, however, before the ladybug came back. Nimblefoot had already grown
anxious. Some misfortune might have befallen her
on the way. So many hungry sparrows were hunting in the woods—their horrible chirping could be
heard everywhere. Nimblefoot almost regretted
having exposed her friend to such dangers.

"Good news! good news!"

It was the ladybug's voice in the air—shrill,

sharp, and excited. Every living thing within ear-
shot looked up curiously. The ladybug landed beside Nimblefoot, scattering her words as fast as
she could pronounce them.

"Nimblefoot, oh, Nimblefoot! In just a day or
two you'll be home! I mean it! All you have to do
is turn back for a little stretch of the road, and
then you'll find a dead birch-tree. You must take
a turn to your left around that tree. There you'll

151

find a wide, well-travelled road that leads straight to the Big Fir. I saw it with my own eyes!"

Nimblefoot came to life again. She leaped to her feet, her eyes shone, and her heart pounded in her breast.

"My old Hustle-Bustle! And you, Brave Heart! Do you hear me?" cried Nimblefoot joyously. "Soon I'll be warming myself at my own hearth, and after such a long journey!"

"Who are those people?" asked the ladybug, perplexed at hearing unfamiliar names. "And I certainly wouldn't want to sit by the hearth on a hot day like this!"

"Well," said Nimblefoot self-consciously, a little ashamed of her sudden outburst. "They're the ones who started me on this journey. And I meant 'hearth' as a kind of picture."

"You mean, as a poetic image," the ladybug corrected her. "Amateurs often confuse such terms. All right, my girl, now we'll just stroll to the nut-bugs' place. They live near that dead birch tree, so you'll actually be farther on your way."

"Fine! Let's go, then," cried Nimblefoot.

Since the ladybug wasn't much of a walker, they agreed to meet at the dead birch tree.

"See you there!" cried the ladybug, circling the clump of wood-sorrel.

Nimblefoot ran along the meandering track, which she recognized as the one she had travelled the day before in the opposite direction. It was strange and wonderful how things were turning out! She felt no more pain in her legs or back. She had become well again, as suddenly as she had fallen sick. Happiness is better medicine than doctors prescribe!

Her reception at the nutbugs' place was very kind. Mr. Nutbug, though he was busy doing the wash, ran out of the house to meet her, waving a diaper and shouting:

"What do my eyes see now? Can it be Nimble-foot? Why, for sure, here she is, at the christening party of our septuplets! An ant at the christening —what a good omen for my little ones' future! Come in, please come right in!"

Three musicians were already there, fiddling away at their lovely melodies, as they rehearsed beneath some tufts of hair-grass. The blades danced in the wind, to the rhythm of the song the musicians were singing at the top of their voices.

Let our joy burn like a fire,
Let us sing a tune of cheer!
And let's banish every care
From the blessed doorstep here.

Now that fortune's benison
Smiles on us from every eye,
Let us sing in unison
Till white dawn fills all the sky!

And tomorrow, while we carry
Troubles down the dusty path,
Let's recall the fiddles' merry
Music, till the autumn's wrath!

The quick tune and gay song excited Nimblefoot. Never had she felt so happy as now.

When the ladybug had recited her verses,
Nimblefoot found them even funnier than before.
She laughed and laughed with the other guests.

"When care and sorrows go, how the heart
sings!" she said to the ladybug. "How right Mr.
Grasshopper was when he told me one rainy day
at Brown Sprinter's house that it's important to
be happy. I didn't understand, then."

"Yes, Nimblefoot, it's true. Anyone who is an
artist knows that. Nothing inspires him so much
as a great sorrow or joy."

"I'm not so sure about the sorrow—," said
Nimblefoot. "But I do like to be happy. Probably
that's because I'm not much of an artist."

"What are you ladies chatting about so much?"
asked a hornet in a gold-colored tunic. Most of

the guests were in military uniforms: army, air force, even some from the navy.

"About you," laughed the ladybug. "We were talking about your sharp sting—which you won't use on us here, though, will you?"

"My sting!" cried the hornet. "They're talking about my sting! But I don't intend to sting anybody at all today!"

"Well! But what about yesterday, when you chased me all around the pussy willows?

"Was it you, Madam? I *am* sorry! But we hadn't been introduced. . ."

"Do you think your sting would have hurt less just because we hadn't met?"

The young hornet gave a charming laugh.

"I wholly disarm myself before these two beautiful young ladies. I realize that my sting is an unfit weapon to win their hearts."

He had become so comically gallant that Nimblefoot laughed more than ever. With a gracious bow, the hornet led the ladybug to a dance. She chattered on as she danced, threatening the hornet with her little finger. Meanwhile the Admiral himself walked over to Nimblefoot. He was handsome in his blue velvet jacket with its rows of white stripes. He stood tall and erect, and had a kindly manner that appealed to Nimblefoot. Her general impression of the Admiral was that of a man she could entirely trust. He looked at Nimblefoot with his dark eyes, and said:

"It would give me great pleasure to dance with you, young lady. You seem so lively! Shall we?"

Nimblefoot took his hand and stepped out on the floor. The Admiral kept giving her compliment after compliment.

"You pirouette as lightly as dandelion fluff. So rarely does one meet an ant at a party! Ants are always so busy, they never find time for entertainment."

"That's our way of life, Admiral," said Nimblefoot. "I didn't expect to be here."

"I've already heard all about your heroic adventures, Miss. I intend to tell your story to my comrades aboard; they'll enjoy it. We sailors love adventure."

"You can hear many stories like mine in these woods," modestly answered Nimblefoot.

"But not about courage like yours, Miss," earnestly answered the Admiral.

It was past midnight when Nimblefoot went to her hosts to wish them and their septuplets good luck. She had intended to leave, but the nutbug would have none of this.

"How can you ever find a place to sleep, out

in the woods, in this darkness? Why, once you're my guest, you must sleep right here in my house!"

And he wouldn't hear Nimblefoot's many protests; he took her to his guest-room under a separate leaf, where a bed had been made for her.

The other guests went on enjoying themselves, and for a long time Nimblefoot heard the music, songs, and laughter through her sleep.

The Admiral did not dance again that night. He talked little, and sat alone for a long time, thinking. Then he drew some lines on a dry grass-blade with one of his long whiskers. Shortly before dawn he called the ladybug and said:

"I've got a map here for Nimblefoot. Would you look at it and check for inaccuracies?"

"My goodness, what a map!" cried the ladybug, surprised. "The wisest bark-beetle couldn't have drawn anything like this, Admiral!"

"Don't let Nimblefoot leave till I come back," he said to the nutbug with a meaningful wink. "Make her wait for me, even if the sun rises before I get back."

And without another word, he walked out.

158

21. IN THE PIRATE'S BOAT

Nimblefoot awoke early. So as not to wake the house, she tiptoed out to the door. There Mrs. Nutbug, who hadn't gone to bed, stopped her.

"I'm not letting you go without breakfast! Who knows, this may be the last time we'll see you. Come on into the dining room, breakfast will be ready in a jiffy."

In the dining room Nimblefoot found the nut-bug and the Poetess. They had gossiped all night and were still at it.

159

"Good morning," said Nimblefoot.

"Good morning," answered the nutbug. "We were waiting for you to get up. We want to go with you part of the way."

"I know you're in a great hurry, Nimblefoot," said the ladybug. "But the Admiral had been rack-ing his brains all night, trying to shorten your way. We must wait for him. Soon he'll be here, he's only checking the map he made for you last night."

As soon as the sun had risen, the Admiral ap-peared. With a bright expression he greeted every-body in his polished manner.

"It's just as I had mapped it out," he said to Nimblefoot. "After crossing the Wide Lake, you can reach the anthill in a few hours. I based my calculations on the average length of step of most ants. You'll be home this very day, Nimblefoot."

"Oh, wonderful!" cried Nimblefoot. "I'm so grateful to you, Admiral!"

"But who'll carry Nimblefoot across the lake?" asked the ladybug.

"I wouldn't be worthy of my admiral's stripes if I hadn't thought of that," replied the Admiral with some pride. "That's why I went to the Landing this morning."

"Not really? Are you taking me on your ship?"

"My ship is due day after tomorrow, and I know

160

you wouldn't like to wait that long," explained the Admiral. "But I've arranged a berth for you on another good vessel. She leaves in a few hours. The Big Fir is on the other side of the Wide Lake, and you'll get there directly by water, instead of overland."

"I suggest you get ready for the crossing," he said. "There's no time to waste—the Captain is already waiting. Miss Ladybug and I will be waiting for you atop the High Reed, which you can see from here. The boat is moored there."

Nimblefoot took leave of the nutbug and his wife and set out to the lakeshore. Following the Admiral's directions, she walked again past the dead birch, turned right, and came down the slope leading to the Wide Lake that would bring her to her native town.

The going was hard; there were no well-travelled tracks. A jungle of grass-roots and mosses, tangled helter-skelter together, blocked her path on every side. Sometimes she had to crawl under the roots. Then, again, she had to climb high above the moss. But she was full of joy and didn't mind the difficulties: she would be home today! It was almost too good to be true.

At last Nimblefoot reached the flatlands and a trail, as the Admiral had said. Now she could travel

much faster. Shortly before noon, through the
thinning grass-blades ahead, Nimblefoot had her
first glimpse of the Wide Lake—a broad green
expanse of still water at the edge of the woods,

known to human beings as the Frog Pond. Nimblefoot paused in surprise and admiration: she had
never seen such a wonderful sight! Impatiently she
ran through the last patch of grass and halted
breathless on the shore, quite near the Landing.

What a noise and crowd were there at the Landing! Thousands of insects, bugs, and beetles—kinds
of which Nimblefoot had never heard, clad in all
sorts of multicolored clothes, were running about,
swimming, or circling in the air; shouting, calling
one another in strange languages; snorting, buzzing, and whistling at the top of their lungs. Loud-
mouthed hawkers pushed through the crowd, calling attention to their wares; sailors in blue jackets,
striped shirts, and bell-bottomed trousers, with
pipes in their mouths, idly ambled along at a
clumsy pace; fliers in blue tunics, with glittering
wings on their shoulders, stood in groups, looking
at the sky. The noise, movement, and kaleidoscope
of colors made Nimblefoot dizzy.

Only after a while did she remember the Admiral and the boat. How was she to find him in
such a tumult? She looked around for the High
Reed that the Admiral had shown her, dim in the
blue haze of the distance. Here it was no different
from the multitude of reeds all along the shore,
each taller than the other.

164

Looking up, she saw a butterfly wandering by. Her four wings were brown, adorned with black spots, and the upper pair was much longer than the lower. And the butterfly was also different from any Nimblefoot had ever seen. She had a long tail of three long, featherlike strips.

"I beg your pardon," said Nimblefoot to the butterfly. "Can you see from up there a ship that's waiting to carry me across the lake?"

"I don't know what a ship is," answered the butterfly indifferently. "I was only born this morning, and I'll die before nightfall."

"Why is your life so short?" asked Nimblefoot, forgetting everything else in her curiosity.

"You've probably never heard about the mayflies, then," said the butterfly. "People call us 'ephemerids.' That's my name, and my life lasts only a day. Tell me, isn't it nice that way? I have no teeth and no stomach, since I'll never eat. And I'll never get bored in my life. Dying, I'll be about as happy as being born. So don't ask me questions —I don't know the answers. I don't even want to know who you are. Farewell."

And she flew away, gracefully moving her four wings.

Nimblefoot stood still, saddened.

"Goodbye, goodbye," she whispered, waving for the last time to her acquaintance.

As she walked along the shore, at last she could distinguish a reed among many others—one that was beyond question the tallest of them all. As she approached, she saw both her friends sitting up on the top.

"Hello!" she cried. "Here I am!"

"Good," the ladybug called down from above. "We were afraid something had happened to you in the jungle."

"Now let me introduce you to the Captain," said the Admiral.

"So, is this my passenger? Very pleased to know you, Miss," said a young sailor aboard a skiff made of a floating leaf. His tunic shone in the sun with all the colors of the rainbow. Nimblefoot easily identified him as a member of the large Spider family. Smaller than most of his relatives, he had very long legs and a yellowish white ribbon sewn all around the collar of his tunic and his coat-tails. Seen from above, on the landing bridge, he looked like the portrait of a real spider, set in a white frame.

"You can go aboard, now," said the Admiral. "Whatever the reputation of the Captain, I promise you, Nimblefoot, that nothing bad will happen to you on the trip. By the way, your Captain is the best sailor on the Wide Lake."

166

Reassured by the Admiral's words, Nimblefoot stepped into the boat, moored by a cobweb to the reed. At once the Captain bit the cable in two, and the ship moved slowly from the shore into the wide green waters stretching out to the horizon.

The Admiral and the ladybug waved from the top of the reed.

"Can you see the Big Fir on the opposite shore? That's your home, Nimblefoot!" cried the ladybug, but Nimblefoot could see nothing but the still expanse of mirrorlike water. Yet she felt so close to home that her heart fluttered with joy.

"Thank you for your kindness, both of you!" she called to the ladybug and the Admiral, as the boat entered the open lake and the reed receded in the distance, now no taller than a grass-blade. A brown dot circled about it—probably the ladybug, on her way home to her willow.

A gentle breeze blew from the shore, pushing the boat ahead at ever-increasing speed. Carefully the Captain scanned the sky all around, then said calmly to Nimblefoot:

"If you see a bird or a dragonfly, hide at once in the cabin," and he showed her a little hut fashioned from a piece of another leaf.

"But there's only room for one in the cabin," said Nimblefoot anxiously. "What will happen to you, Captain?"

"Never mind me," he laughed. "I'll dive under the boat and hang onto the keel. I have enough air in my lungs to last me at least a half hour."

"Really? Then you're ready for anything," said Nimblefoot. "But does that happen very often?"

"Oh, quite a few times a day," he said light-heartedly. "Dangers are everywhere, especially at sea. This isn't the land, where you can hide in any nook or cranny."

"How often do you cross the lake?"

"Usually twice a day, if the wind's favorable. That's how I make a living."

"What fare do you charge your passengers?" asked Nimblefoot, blushing as she remembered she had no money.

"Nothing; I'm not a carrier, mind you. I earn my living as a lifeguard," answered the Captain a little self-consciously, avoiding her eyes.

Then he turned away, scanned the distance, whistled between his teeth, and began to sing in a fine baritone:

> Again I sail across wide seas,
> Above the hidden depths, the dark!
> Oh, drive me onward, on, fair breeze,
> Wherever fortune steers my bark!

But he had no time to finish his song. Quickly he jumped onto the lake and ran over its surface

as easily as on land. His inflatable boots kept the Captain above water. Nimblefoot soon saw what he had meant by calling himself a lifeguard. Not far away a fly was struggling for her life in the water. In a few strides the Captain was at her side; he picked her up and carried her in his arms to the boat.

Nimblefoot marvelled at how quick he was. She moved aside to make room for the poor fly to lie down and dry her wings in the sun. But the Captain did not climb aboard; instead, he dived with his rescue straight under the boat. Only after a while did he surface—alone.

"Forgive me for leaving you," he said, jumping

into the boat. "I had to take action in the line of duty."

He sat down, as calm as if nothing had happened, and looked across the lake shimmering in the sunshine.

Naturally, Nimblefoot couldn't control her curiosity.

"But why did you dive? I couldn't see any danger," she said.

"There wasn't any," he replied.

"But—where's the fly? The one you saved?"

The Captain gave Nimblefoot a blank stare.

"You scoundrel—you ate her!"

"Well," said the Captain, unruffled. "Whatever you call it, I did save her from the jaws of a frog."

"But how could that help the poor little fly?"

"Why, don't you see? Would you rather be swallowed by an old, slimy frog, or by a young, gallant sailor who's a pirate Captain to boot?"

"Then—am I on a pirate vessel?"

"Of course. If you like that word better than another."

"Did the Admiral know this?"

"Certainly he did, Miss."

Nimblefoot shrank from him so sharply that the Captain felt a need to reassure her.

"But I'd starve rather than think of touching

a passenger! The Admiral knew me well enough to entrust you to me. Yes, I'm a pirate. But I have my own code of honor. I eat only those who'll otherwise drown or be swallowed by frogs. I have as much right as any frog to use anything and any-one that fate throws into the sea. Right?"

Nimblefoot didn't answer. She only knew that she was at the mercy of a pirate, who had no real pity at all.

"No use arguing about our different ways of life, Miss," said the Captain as he again jumped into the water, this time to "save" a mushroom-bug who was thrashing about in the water. Nimblefoot closed her eyes, revolted by what was bound to follow.

She sat for a long time with her eyes shut, until the boat began to sway and dip wildly. Nimble-foot looked up and saw they were approaching the opposite shore, dancing over the ripples of surf. Before her eyes the woods emerged, shimmering in the sultry summer afternoon. The breeze, blowing off-shore, carried the spicy aroma of flowers and honey. Farther off, in the woods, she saw a tall fir that stood out from the other trees—it must be the Big Fir that sheltered her town! Nimblefoot paid no more attention to the Captain. She stared at the Big Fir, all her thoughts now of home.

The boat shot over the surf and struck the shore, quivering from bow to stern.

"We've arrived, Miss Ant," said the Captain, jumping ashore.

He seized the prow, and expertly moored the boat to a grass root.

Nimblefoot thanked him courteously for the ride and sprang out. The Captain gave her a smart military salute.

"Please excuse anything painful that may have happened during the trip," he said.

"That's all right," she said curtly, reassured as soon as her feet touched the land. "And thank you for not swallowing me!"

The Captain pretended not to have heard her.

"I wish you a pleasant walk home," he said good-naturedly. "As soon as the wind changes, I'll sail back to the Landing. It's a pleasure to be out on the lake in such beautiful weather. Sometimes, when the storms set in, I have to stay at the Landing a whole week, and I starve. Anyway, the land's not for me. My heart draws me to the sea. And my stomach, to tell the truth. . . On a day like this, I eat enough to last me a week!"

As he went on talking, Nimblefoot made her way into the woods, her eyes fixed on the Big Fir, her guidepost.

22. RETURN OF THE NATIVE ANT

Unaware, Nimblefoot quickened her pace till she was running without a pause for breath. Even so, after her experience with the ant lion, she moved with caution. She examined every suspicious patch of sand before venturing onto it, and tested every grass-tuft with her feelers. Why risk her life so close to home? She avoided every hole and ditch—even the roots of trees, where a murderer could dart out and drag her into a dark cave.

The sun was setting when Nimblefoot climbed over a fallen tree and halted in amazement: before her, skirting the trunk, ran a wide, well-paved road. Nimblefoot touched it with her antennae, sniffed the pebbles, and cried out joyously:

"This is the highway to my town!"

And she was right. It was the main road, paved by the town engineers, which led from the woods and fields straight into the anthill. Nimblefoot hurried to the center of the road and began to run at tremendous speed. What smooth going it was!

"I'm home, home," she repeated to herself, forgetting the hardships and dangers she had overcome, and the harsh slavery that had been the only life she had once known.

"Hey! What's the hurry?" asked a voice behind her in the black ant language. "Can't even catch you! What do you mean, coming home empty-handed?"

Nimblefoot turned and saw a little black ant, just like herself, who was carrying a heavy burden on her back.

"My sister!" cried Nimblefoot, embracing her.

"What's the matter with you? Did someone scare you?" asked the ant in astonishment. "Are you sick?"

"No, I'm not!" replied Nimblefoot. "But I'm coming home from the castle of the red ants, where I was born and where I was a slave. That's why I'm empty-handed. I'm bringing with me only a full, homesick heart."

"Well, if all that's true, you're bringing back a lot more than I am," answered the black ant, her eyes widening. She threw down her burden and opened her bread-pouch.

"You look half starved, and your hands are shaking. You must be tired, too. Here, eat first, and then tell me your story."

Meanwhile, more ants turned up on their way back from the fields. Filled with wonder, all of them stopped and crowded around. Who had ever heard of a slave escaping and making it back from the red ants?

"Let's not waste time," said one. "The Queens must be told about this."

At the gate, where everyone was checked in since the attack of the red ants, a soldier halted Nimblefoot.

"I don't know you. Who are you?"

"I'm Nimblefoot, back from captivity, and I bring greetings to everyone from Hustle-Bustle, our old nurse!"

"What! Can it be possible?" cried the officer of the guard, who stood nearby. And, seizing Nimblefoot's waist in his powerful hands, he swung her around in the air, shouting with joy:

"Little one, you're an example to all of us old soldiers!"

Notified of Nimblefoot's return, the Queens called a special meeting that same evening. Nimblefoot told them her story from beginning to end. She repeated what she had heard from Brave Heart about Iron Jaw. And she suggested that the red ant Leader might be exchanged for Hustle-Bustle and the other slaves, if he were alive.

That night a search party of miners and soldiers went down into the underground winter quarters to look for Iron Jaw. They found him alive, though gray-bearded, haggard, and reduced to a skeleton. They also found two of his adjutants, one unconscious—though he revived after a long drink of cold water.

The rescued were fed, then placed under guard by a strong detachment of elite troops. The next day, official messengers of the Queens set forth on a journey to the castle of the red ants, with news of Iron Jaw's rescue, and a letter signed by the robber Leader himself.

Nimblefoot became the heroine of her home town. All spoke of her courage and skill, and exchanged tales of her adventures. So many wanted to speak to her, shake hands with her, or at least see her, that the Queens had to place her under guard in a secret room.

The messengers reached the castle of the robbers on the evening of the next day, and presented Iron Jaw's letter. They advised the robbers to meet the conditions set forth by the Queens. If these were fulfilled, Iron Jaw would be returned to his castle.

The conditions were harsh. The robbers had not only to release all their slaves at once; they had to promise to leave the town of the black ants absolutely in peace, thereafter. The Council of Nobles called all the robbers to a meeting, to decide what action to take.

The robbers had already learned that they were helpless without Iron Jaw. Their state was about to collapse in discord. After a long, sometimes violent debate, they voted to accept the terms of the exchange. The slaves were released; escorted by red ant soldiers, they were sent back to their kinsmen, the black ants.

How happy Nimblefoot was to see her old nurse

back, safe and sound! She ran far down the road to meet the friends of her captive days, and she wept with joy as she embraced Hustle-Bustle.

"Who could have expected such a happy end?" sighed the old nurse, embracing her little ant.

In the black ant town, Iron Jaw signed the articles of exchange, written on a gnat's wing, wiped the sweat from his brow, and politely took leave of the Council of Queens. The guards took him outside to the robber escort, which had of course not been admitted within the gates.

Many ants had gone out for their last look at the famous robbers. Nimblefoot, who hoped to see Brave Heart, was among them. She had so much to tell about her trip home! But he was not there. As Hustle-Bustle explained to her later, Brave Heart was no longer alive.

"He died a hero's death, Nimblefoot, defending the black ant slaves out in the fields, when they were assaulted by unknown marauders from the woods. He was carried home with a deep wound in his chest. He called out your name before he died. And he asked me to tell you, if I saw you, that he was glad to give up his life for others."

"He was a true hero," said Nimblefoot, wiping her eyes. "And I shall always cherish him in my memory."

179

180

A new life began for Nimblefoot—the peaceful, happy life of a black ant in a busy community.

The town grew and prospered, to become the largest and most important anthill in the woods. It stands under the Big Fir today. But it would be hard to find. The branches of the tree hide it from strangers' eyes, and protect it like the hands of a mother.

Nimblefoot, today an old lady, often describes her adventures to the young ants, who listen to her breathlessly.

Her voice trembles when she speaks of the young robber, Brave Heart, who died a hero, with no less honor than the old nurse Hustle-Bustle. Like her, he too chose a life and death of self-sacrifice.

OTHER PUBLICATIONS BY MANYLAND BOOKS, INC.

Francisco Coloane: THE STOWAWAY. Translated from the Spanish by Adele Breaux. Illustrated by John J. Floherty, Jr. 114 pages. Cloth. $3.00.

Nola M. Zobarskas, ed.: THE MOUNTAIN DOVES and Other African Folk Tales. Illustrated by Pranas Lapé. 137 pages. Cloth. $3.50

Clarence R. Decker and Charles Angoff, eds.: MODERN STORIES FROM MANY LANDS. *The Literary Review Book.* (Stories from Austria, Chile, Greece, India, Indonesia, Ireland, Israel, Italy, Japan Netherlands, Philippines, Turkey, United States of America). 316 pages. Cloth. $5.00.

Ignas Šeinius: THE ORDEAL OF ASSAD PASHA. A Novella. Translated from the Lithuanian by Raphael Sealey. 61 pages. Cloth. $2.00.

Jurgis Gliauda: HOUSE UPON THE SAND. A novel. Translated from the Lithuanian by Raphael Sealey and Milton Stark. 168 pages. Cloth. $3.95.

Stepas Zobarskas, ed.: SELECTED LITHUANIAN SHORT STORIES. 280 pages. Cloth. $5.00.

Stepas Zobarskas, ed.: LITHUANIAN QUARTET. Sample works by four modern Lithuanian authors: Aloyzas Baronas, Marius Katiliškis, Algirdas Landsbergis, and Ignas Šeinius. 212 pages. Cloth. $4.95.